Praise for *Out of Her Backp*

"[These stories] are well-written in a no-nonsense, nitty-gritty style, evoking the sights, tastes, and smells of exotic locales . . ."

~*Victoria Times Colonist*

"A refreshingly different read. . . . Cutler shows life as it is, complete with cramped overnight train rides, food poisoning, and the ever-present fear of trusting the wrong person or taking the wrong, ill-fated bus."

~Carolyn Ali, *Georgia Straight*

"A distinctly Canadian view of travelling by the seat of the pants . . . Cutler travelled the world . . . adding critical depth of detail to the exotic settings."

~Mike Youds

Jumping Off

Jumping Off

Laura J. Cutler

National Library of Canada Cataloguing in Publication Data
Cutler, Laura, 1966–
Jumping off / Laura J. Cutler.

ISBN 1-896300-59-6

I. Title.
PS8555.U8464J85 2003   C813'.6   C2003-910008-1
PR9199.4.C87J85 2003

Editor for the Press: Lynne Van Luven
Cover and interior design: Ruth Linka
Cover image: Getty Images
Author photo: James Matheson

"The Full Brazilian" was originally published in *3 A.M.*, Winter 2001.
"Something to Justify the Day" was originally published in
Bathtub Gin, Spring/Summer 2000.

NeWest Press acknowledges the support of the Canada Council for the Arts, the Alberta Foundation for the Arts and the Edmonton Arts Council for our publishing program. We also acknowledge the financial support of the Government of Canada through the Book Publishing Industry Development Program (BPIDP) for our publishing activities.

NeWest Press
201–8540–109 Street
Edmonton, Alberta
T6G 1E6
(780) 432-9427
www.newestpress.com

1   2   3   4   5   07   06   05   04   03

PRINTED AND BOUND IN CANADA

For Jamie again,

because there is no other.

Contents

The Third Tryst

"What would you say if I drizzled honey all over you, then slowly licked it off?"

"I'd say, 'Don't even think about kissing me, not with a mouthful of honey.'" She says it a little sharply because he already knows this. He should know it, after that time at Denny's when he thought he'd been doing her a favour by smearing her toast with golden *miel* while she was off hunting down a ketchup bottle for the home fries.

"Well, what then?" Nate says merrily, and she wonders why he's bothering to act so playful. The weekend has already been ruined, rendered as unsalvageable as used tissue, thanks to her brief foray into honesty. Apparently honesty was no virtue. "What then? Ketchup?" he presses, perhaps inspired by the too-late Denny's memory. "Gyro sauce," he suggests, and she refuses to acknowledge the innuendo.

Nate finishes, sounding rather triumphant, with, "Soy sauce?"

Carolyn grimaces. "Only if you want to lick hives off me." He knows this too, about the allergy, jokes all the time about how she can consider herself Chinese, with an allergy like that. Depending on her mood, she may tartly remind him that she is Canadian. Second-generation. On good days, she might quip, "Two chicks, two chicks, two chicks in one." Right now she's on middle ground and finally, half-heartedly, smiles. "Try red-wine gravy."

"Blech." He starts to tickle her, and it quickly and distinctly leads to passion. His.

"Sorry. Can you move? I have to pee." She extracts herself from the crumpled white sheet, his baboon limbs, his pouchy eyes, and moves into the bathroom.

It is a standard, economy motel bathroom. The towels are neither luxurious nor plentiful. There are, however, many teeny bars of waxy soap in shiny paper. There are two acrylic glasses wrapped in crisp paper. There were. They have been stripped and now hold the dregs of gin. A more efficient receptacle for their potent concoctions, Carolyn thinks, would have been the plastic ice bucket.

She leans over to scratch off the last island of ice-blue polish from her left big toe. Some of the marks on the linoleum are décor; some are the result of runaway cigarettes. Some are deliberate scores from delinquent penknives, while still others are indistinguishable and disconcerting stains. She winces at the fluorescent light, invasive as a speculum.

why am I here.

She is ponytailing her coarse black hair—it feels like greasy spaghetti—and cursing Nate for getting massage oil in it, when she hears him pad across the room.

"What do you feel like eating?" He leans against the bathroom doorframe, naked unless his cigarette counts. He has no self-consciousness, no awareness, even, of his narrow shoulders, his slight paunch. She is grateful that he is off of sex and onto another, more banal, hunger.

"Not pizza." She is definite. One of them has to be body-conscious. "Nothing heavy. Ummm, spinach salad, clear soup."

"Oysters?" he pipes in hopefully.

Carolyn forces a laugh but doesn't answer. She wants to pop the large zit weighting down her jaw but cannot, obviously, do so in his presence; they have just progressed to urinating in front of each other, and only when tipsy. She keeps fussing with the barrette, her glossy black eyes boring into their mirrored twins. Finally, Nate pushes off the doorframe and leaves her in peace. His ass is gray-white, the colour of her grandmother's *congee*.

Strangely, Carolyn thinks about Jason, at home alone. In their Kits condo. She thinks about the comfort of snuggling into him on the couch, of sharing mundane stories; she considers their quick but affectionate sex—though lately, she is far more familiar with Nate's contours and how they fit with her own. She gulps water from the tap to weigh down the thoughts.

Already, they'd lost four hours of precious time while Nate sulked out her tentative suggestion to cut their tryst short. Christ, it was only a suggestion, a small appetizer of the truths she wanted to serve up. It took sex, a backrub, and thirty minutes of Australian Rules Football on TSN to pull him out of it. As the Melbourne commentator drawled on, she'd thought, God, you're not handsome. Not even cute. Jason, at least, always had the dimples and a redhead's freckles to see him through harsh lights and harsh times.

why am I here.

"Why don't you go pick something up?" Carolyn calls out, as she listens to him pulling on slacks and snapping out his crisp sweatshirt before pulling it over his head. Suddenly, getting him away is more important than eating light.

I'd like to cancel my Nate-lite, please.

"Noooooo," he blubbers playfully. "I want you to come with me."

"Please, Nate? Remember, I need to call home and you know I can't do it with you in the room, so please?"

He groans. "Fine. Kick me out. If I didn't know better . . ."

". . . you'd think I was calling one of my other lovers," she finishes for him wryly. Old standard. "Get anything, but not too heavy. Okay? Nothing heavy."

When she sees he has rounded the east wing of the motel, headed toward the nearest cluster of food joints, Carolyn uses her cellphone to call her husband. It only makes sense to use the cellphone; they have call display at home. She is supposed to be in Seattle, supervising the installation of a new Clinique cosmetics counter at some mall. Carolyn has not ridden out two and nine-tenths affairs undetected because she is careless.

"Hi, hun," she greets.

"Hi. How're you doing? How are the Seattle Clinettes?" Carolyn laughs out loud at their private reference to the Clinique counter-girls.

"Okay, they're okay. Boppy." A huge risk here: "Listen, I might be able to make it home early. You'll be around?"

"Of course! But why? How early?"

She tenses momentarily. Sometimes Jason doesn't care whether she has been to the moon or the sun, but sometimes he's a stickler for details. It is most inconvenient, when he asks innocent questions about her lies. "I'll let you know if it's sometime weird; otherwise, I'll just see you when I see you." Anxious to change the subject, Carolyn asks, "So, what are you doing now?"

"Eating popcorn, watching the tube." Suddenly, she is aware of both background noises. "Trying to study my Mandarin so I'm ready for New Year's and your grandmother."

Grandmother. Her body fifty-two years in Vancouver, her soul still in Beijing, she'd just as soon go to her grave as acknowledge Jason. His whiteness. His non-Asian-ness. *You marry Chinese boy, Wu Chia, not white boy. Chinese boy have honour, not so, white boy.*

Yes, Grandmother. Very honourable, the way the young dragon dancer had managed to cop a good feel of her sixteen-year-old vagina before the Tai Chi class started. She thought they were just going to kiss. Most honourable.

"And what are you doing? How come you're not out drinking with the gals?" Jason. Talking. Concentrate.

Though she is alone in the room, Carolyn waves her free hand around vaguely to punctuate her point. "Oh, well, you know . . . I guess I'm tired."

"Okay. I'll let you go. Be good . . ."

". . . and if I can't be good?" she interrupts, rather snappishly, and he is caught off guard.

"Uh, I dunno. Be careful? Be awesome?"

"Goodnight, Jason."

"Love you!"

"Luvyoutoo." She says it fast because Nate will expect something similar during the evening, and it's excruciating to proffer sentiments to her husband and her lover, back to back. Carolyn's one girlfriend who knows of the infidelities is perversely fascinated by the idea of sex with two men within twelve hours. Hell, once it was unavoidably within three. As much as Carolyn tries to avoid such couplings, the verbal demands are far more difficult.

the demands on the soul.

Nate brings back aluminum containers of mushroom chop suey, chicken fried rice, and slices of barbequed pork. Grandmother would refuse to eat such bastardized dishes. Carolyn claims the vegetables. She gained twelve pounds during the months with Lance because they were always eating cheese-smothered burritos. That consequence alone had been enough to make the inevitable split relatively easy. Conversely, the week with the broker had been pure alcohol, not one bite of food, not even on pretense.

Food choices are an area where Nate usually gets points. That, plus he is a damn fine lover, despite his pasty, hound-dog appearance. And he is keen on holistic health and shopping, the activities that fill their hours between raucous fucks during these sporadic getaways. The majority of life-hours are filled with their respective spouses, doing prosaic things like buying groceries and sorting laundry and visiting in-laws.

"So, when can you get away again?" Nate asks, popping his last flaccid squiggle of pork into her mouth. She gums it, suddenly full, though she has only picked at her chop suey. "Let's make it soon, baby," he purrs.

let's not.

"I don't know. But yeah, soon." She moves to clear the vestiges from the bed. Little chores such as this are her primary avoidance technique. Others include returning towels to bathrooms, mad searches through overnight bags for birth control pills, runs for ice, and of course, copious pees.

"Promise you'll try?"

"Mmmm."

He will not be dissuaded. "You know, we should think about going somewhere real, not just a cheesy motel. Vegas, maybe? Maybe that little German village in Washington State. LaConner, is it?"

Carolyn is frequently overwhelmed in Nate's presence. The way he pushes for time and sex and soul, it is frequently over-whelming. This time, however, she becomes angry at his fervour.

She turns away from him. "It's not going to happen, Nate."

"Oh, baby, don't say that. You'll find a way; you always do. Make some sacrifices. Do you know how many I make for us? Shit, *gladly* make, but still . . . for instance, it's Shelley's birthday this weekend; did you know that?"

"How could I know that?" She feels vulnerable in the nude and yanks on a T-shirt. It smells like banana oil, and she gags.

"Well, I wasn't going to tell you, because obviously I chose to be with you."

"But you're telling me now that it's your wife's birthday. As a punishment. What do you expect me to feel?"

Now they are both tight with irritation. There is no more gin. The depressive effects of their earlier imbibing could not have hit at a worse time.

"I don't expect you to feel anything," Nate retorts. She knows he is trying to sound bewildered, like he's tasting her ambiguity for the first time, but the words come out too clipped. He starts slamming around the room for his smokes. "Why are you being like this?"

"Like what?" Carolyn challenges.

by all means, tell me what the hell I'm doing, being, feeling.

"Peevish. Ungrateful. Selfish. Captious." Nate is never lost for words. Still, Grandmother's indecipherable Mandarin invectives against her children, grandchildren, fate, and life are more cutting. Carolyn wishes she'd learned Mandarin and could now lash out at Nate with the force of the Yangtze tidal bore.

Regardless, this is the turning point. With Lance, it came in his Volvo, halfway across the Second Narrows Bridge; with the broker, it was in a bar of course, five minutes before she was due home to prepare hors d'heurves for twenty colleagues from Jason's engineering firm. It had almost happened at least five times with Nate as well, though he pretends he doesn't know it.

Carolyn is proud that she drives any and all discussions like an Indy 500 racer, able to swerve in an instant, if need be. As deftly as Grandmother and her cronies playing mah-jong.

"Well, those are lovely sentiments, stellar qualities in a person," she snarls in response to Nate's adjectives as she wrenches on her jeans. "Why the hell are you here then, if I'm so incredibly ignorant?"

"I wonder."

gear down, Schumacher.

So calmly, she says, "Funny you should say that, because I too have been 'wondering' for quite some time. I'll stop now, as the answer is clear."

Nate suddenly looks stricken, so Carolyn busies herself throwing items into her carryall—earrings, a tube of facial scrub from the bathroom, her pink toothbrush, and other minute pieces of her feminine presence. When she goes back into the bathroom to make a final visual sweep, she says loudly, because she doesn't want to repeat it, "I need to concentrate on my marriage for a while. This constant double-header being played in my head is, well, I don't like it." She emerges and sloughs into her jacket.

where are you going to go, stupid?

"Besides," she injects slyly, suddenly unwilling to shoulder all the blame of being the one that ended it, "it seems apropos, since you were thinking it too."

During this short altercation, Nate's eyes have become even droopier, his lips thinner, his jowls more pronounced. This is what Carolyn sees, anyway. She feels freed and is pulsing with new energy. She gets the same vitality at the trysts' beginnings. She slips back the security chain that Nate compulsively uses in each motel room they share, as if it will stop the entrance of an irate Jason or a hysterical Shelley. Her hand is on the doorknob.

I wanna hear you beg.

"When I said, 'I wonder why I'm with you,' I was being sarcastic." He grips her face and yanks her close. "I don't wonder, ever, Carolyn. I love you."

She retracts her hand from the knob and lets the bag thunk to the floor. It's true that she has nowhere else to go tonight; it's already 10:30, and she is supposed to be three-plus hours from Vancouver by rental car, not twenty minutes by SkyTrain.

They stand, frozen, for several moments before Carolyn leans in, almost imperceptibly. It's enough for Nate, and he crumples into her.

Carolyn stares over Nate's shoulder and concentrates on the framed and compulsory copy of the Innkeeper's Act, which is screwed to the wall. She will stay the night; it's good enough to know she will extricate herself from this third tryst in the morning.

"I'm sorry, baby," says Nate. "I don't mean to push. You just don't understand how much I want you."

"Ummm," Carolyn allows.

"I love you," says Nate again, clearly and forcefully into her ear.

"Ummhmm."

Carolyn shifts her gaze to her abandoned dinner. It sits on the desk, an unappetizing pile in a congealed sauce.

White Muslim

The day my mother met me for lunch in Pacific Centre Mall's food court, my head was swathed in soft muslin, traditional Islamic style. An *isharb*. She dropped her red melamine tray. The clatter was audible above some piped-in rapper's butchering of "Do You Hear What I Hear?" and pork fried rice spit into the air in all directions.

"You're doing it; you've done it. Oh, my child," she whispered after crossing herself and sitting down. It was selfish of me to confirm one of her worst nightmares in public like that, but I just couldn't have handled it on more intimate territory.

It started over a year ago, in her very own foyer.

"Ma, this is Halil, the man I told you about."

"Hello, Halil," said my mother brightly, extending her hand. She'd been amply warned to expect his deep-brown chestnut eyes, his broad, strong features, his—I'd grasped to describe it—

Mediterranean-like complexion. Comparative pepper to our family's salty whiteness. "Welcome to our home. Come in." I sensed her gushy tone change slightly when she called, "David! David, come out. The kids are here."

"Twenty-nine years old, and we're still 'the kids,'" I muttered nervously.

Halil smiled benignly and squeezed my shoulder. "That's an international mom thing; don't worry."

We settled around the four corners of the living room—better, I supposed, than a two-on-two faceoff. Halil requested apple juice, and my father frowned. Men did not come over to his house on a Saturday night to drink apple juice. Scotch, vodka at least, was an acceptable drink. Strangely, in their glasses, the amber liquids were visually interchangeable.

But not the men drinking them.

When I too refused my usual white wine, his eyes opened and I could see the wheels turn in his head. Only pregnant women turned down alcohol. I let him stew. My mother sipped sherry from her usual thimble-sized glass.

"So, Halil, Deborah has told us so little of you, but I understand you're an orthopedic surgeon?"

Halil flashed his prize-winning smile. Jesus, that guy's handsome, I reflected, then mentally kicked myself.

No. Not Jesus.

"Yes, Mrs. Piscia, uh, Sofia," he corrected when she started to protest. "Yes, Sofia, that I am."

"And so young," murmured my mother, her thoughts offered up for public viewing as well.

"Remember I told you Halil perfected a new technique for replacing vertebrae? The actual name's impossible to remember, but I think it should be called a Halilectomy." The three of us had a polite chuckle while my father frowned on.

"And you must be proud of Deborah," said Halil graciously. "Teaching is a most noble profession in my mother country."

"Really, I thought your heroes were . . ."

"Daddy," I interrupted, not trusting his commentary but desperate to include him in this inaugural meeting, "Halil is practically a professional mechanic. He loves tinkering under hoods, just like you."

My father grunted. I had known this wouldn't be easy, but he was bordering on rude. We made small talk despite him until my mother jumped up to get some snacks.

"David, come help."

A smile pulled at my lips: she was taking him into the kitchen for one of her famous AAs—Attitude Adjustments—like he was a sullen teen.

"So, how do you think it's going?" Halil quietly asked after they'd left the living room, his baritone voice delightfully spiced with a Saudi accent but no trace of nervousness.

"As expected, I guess. I just hope we don't have to go the distance tonight. I want them to get to know you as a person first. I want them . . ." I swallowed to rid my throat of its inexplicable fig-sized obstruction, and rolled my eyes in response to the tears that welled. "I want them to come to know you as the man I love."

"And are going to marry?" he added, playfully patting his jacket pocket, where I'd felt compelled to thrust my brand-new engagement ring before my mother had answered the door.

"Yes, Halil, who I will marry."

Somebody's god was looking out for me that night, as it passed without incident. Without the need to fully disclose . . . everything.

The second time my parents met Halil, they had us over for Sunday dinner, a former family mainstay. For the first time in ages, my sister, brother, their respective spouses, and growing clans simultaneously appeared at my mother's mahogany table. My older sister Raquel whispered to me over the shrimp cocktail, "Word has it this one's serious," and jerked her thumb in Halil's direction. I made a juvenile face at her and stabbed an errant piece of lettuce to avoid both her insinuations and my father, who this time blatantly squinted at my stomach when I declined a drink.

Get used to it, Deb.

Dinner got difficult after the shrimp cocktail starters, when my mother announced she'd made baked pork chops, a dish of which she's particularly proud and which no one ever refuses. Granted, it was my fault: I should have told her we didn't eat pork. Halil never had, and I hadn't since we'd become engaged.

"It's okay," I cajoled when she started fussing. "We'll double-up on vegetables. And rice. There's enough rice to feed a village." Halil's knee pressed against mine under the table, a gentle caution not to raise my voice in volume or pitch. He's good that way. "Really, Ma. It's fine. And I'm sorry I didn't tell you. Please stop saying you're embarrassed."

My brother-in-law's comment was a mixed blessing. "So, Halil," he said bluntly between mouthfuls of the famous mushroom-souped chops, "does this mean you're a practising Muslim?"

There was a painfully long pause; in theatre, I think it's called a pregnant pause. The three kids weren't paying attention, as they were too wrapped up in bantering about Pokemon's comeback, but always one for controversy, my sister actually grinned. My parents, whose knowledge of Islam was limited to what they occasionally heard on the six o'clock news, could not hide their fearful

expressions. I surmised that they were wondering if Halil was carrying a Molotov cocktail or would suddenly start chanting in
Arabic and upstage my brother's litany of one-liners.

"Yes," answered Halil steadfastly. Then, "Yes, we are Muslim."

If the first pause was pregnant, the second was a few months
overdue.

"I beg your pardon, but who?" asked my mother finally.

"Shit," breathed my sister.

"I think you mean Shiite," smiled Halil, but no one got the
joke except me.

"Who's Muslim?" interjected my mother again, far more
forcefully this time.

"We are," I answered, with more bravado than I felt.

"No," clarified my mother slowly and carefully, like we were
all children in the after-school art classes she leads. "Your friend
Halil might be Muslim, but you, Deborah, are Catholic. Cath-o-
lic," she emphasized. Then, realizing her less-than-graciousness in
her ever-gracious home, she rearranged her face into sculptured
pleasantness, like she does when Father Duncan speaks about car-
nal ("Jeepers Ma, just say sex, will ya?") relations during Mass. "It's
nice to have friends of different persuasions."

My brother snorted. "Not persuasions, Ma. That's like gays, as
in sexual persuasions."

"Daniel, we're at the table," said my mother and sister at exactly
the same time, though Raquel's counter dripped with glee.

"It's time, Deborah," prompted Halil quietly.

I stared into the casserole dish of glistening pork chops.
"Mom, Dad, Raquel and Jacques, Daniel and Susan: Halil isn't just
my friend—isn't, actually, even my boyfriend. I love him, and we're
getting married next year."

"Whoa!" bellowed Daniel as his wife, Susan, let out a supportive squeal. Raquel whistled and Jacques developed a sudden interest in his kids' leftover carrot medallions. Dad sawed away at what I knew was a perfectly tender chop, and my mother starting clearing plates that people were still eating off of.

"Ma?"

"Who'd like dessert?" she spluttered, stacking far too many shapes and sizes of dishes on one arm. "I've got apple pie or cupcakes from the spring bazaar. Now, they've been frozen, but Maria Contras made them, so they should be . . ."

"Ma, please sit down. Things aren't coming out right," I pleaded to her ceramic-like face, which both frightened and exasperated me. She sat stiffly on the edge of her chair.

"So, what, you'll be wearing one of those big black things?" she sniffed. "Quite the change from the little tart that tried sneaking out her bedroom window in a borrowed leather miniskirt and rib-tickler."

Raquel's jaw dropped at my mother's utterance of tart out of its baked-goods context.

"Ma, I was fifteen years old, and it's not the same at all. The big *blue* things are burquas and um, generally only worn in Afghanistan because of the Taliban. The women are made to wear them out of political strife, not religion." I kind of hiccuped, wishing I'd researched Islamic dress further. A traditional Saudi wife was mostly covered too. "All a woman is required to do under Qu'ran teaching is dress with modesty. Especially a Western one, like me. Right, Halil?" He flicked his eyes subtly, knowing his backing was irrelevant, perhaps even detrimental.

I plowed on. "Okay, yes, I will cover my head in mosque, just like our Italian ancestors did for Mass." My mother couldn't refute this; we had pictures of squat, swathed women coming out of a Florence cathedral.

At that moment, Sarah, one of Raquel's kids, split her lip open when she tripped on the kitchen mat and slammed into Ma's pristine tile, so I was spared further inquisitions.

Halil and I prepared to leave shortly thereafter. I received the scantiest of kisses before being bade goodnight.

I met my mother for a private lunch later that week at a suburban Keg restaurant. She was playing with the folds of the napkin so fervently that I was compelled to gently press her hands into her lap. "Ma," I tried, "why did you marry Daddy?"

She looked at me with irritation and then answered, rankled already, "Because I loved him, of course."

"And I love Halil. He loves me."

She shook her head. "No, it's not the same."

Serenity, I intoned, my limited collection of Arabic prayers having flown from my mind. "It *is* the same. I love him. He's kind, funny, intelligent and caring and handsome and committed to healing people. What more could I ask for?"

"That he be at least Anglican," she snapped, snatching up her napkin again. "Even Baptist, though they don't understand the importance of Easter enough. Lent and all. Just not this Muslin stuff."

"Muslim," I corrected automatically and she threw me a withering glance. We were silent, holding neutral expressions while the server removed our plates.

In barely a whisper, she said, "But I brought you up Catholic. You are Catholic, Deborah Maria. It would be like taking blood from a stone." Then she tried blatant racism. "Really, Deborah, anything but those people."

Horrified, I stage-whispered back, "'*Those* people'? Ma!" I glugged the last of my iced-tea. "They believe in God, Ma, only the messenger is different." I struggled to solidify what was still jelly in my own mind. "Instead of Christ, I believe the ultimate messenger is Mohammed. But one God, Ma. I still believe in one ultimate God."

"I just don't know how I'll be able to face anyone," she faltered.

"Anyone *who*?" I countered instantly, my vows of peace abandoned.

"Everyone."

"Church people," I answered for her.

She accepted a coffee refill with a grim smile for the waiter, who seemed to sense it was in his best interest to make a fast getaway. "In part. Plus your relatives. The people at the club. They won't listen to all these wonderful explanations you're giving me. They hear foreign names like Mohammed and run like the dickens."

The coffee was very bitter, it seemed to me. "That's their problem. I promise to still buy spring daffodils from Mrs. B., and go hear the kids sing in the choir."

She eyed me suspiciously. "You'd be allowed? I wouldn't have thought that."

Exasperated, I said loudly, "Ma, it's a way of life, not a cult." Diners from several tables glanced over anxiously, and I forced my voice down. "It's a way of living and thinking, like the way you do some things because you're Italian, some things because Nana's Irish. Just please stop with the stereotypes and assumptions."

She looked mollified, and I reached out to squeeze her hand. "Remember, you're not losing a daughter; you're gaining forty per cent of the world's belief." This was a made-up number, but I thought it sounded reasonable.

"One more question, then I must get going."

I squared my shoulders and took a calming breath. "Ummm?"

"What about covering your head? Tell me about that again. You've such pretty hair, the only one who got the fair Irish genes. Those women," she paused and self-corrected, "such women cover their heads, you know, burqua or no burqua. And they don't wear short sleeves or even knee-length skirts. It makes them look so browbeaten."

"Ma, that's like, the least important aspect of the whole thing, but no, I won't be. Halil and I talked about it. Remember, he's been in Canada for years now and lived in London before that. We've talked very carefully about what is religion, what is culture, and what is politics. You pass dozens of women on the street every day that follow Islam, and you don't even realize it."

Her mouth was still set in a tight line, but she nodded slowly. I told her I loved her and we parted ways.

After that, things really got ugly and complicated.

"Ma, Dad, I have exciting but difficult news to tell you."

We'd invited them over for Sunday brunch, and I hoped the fluffy eggs florentine would soften the blow. Their forks froze midway to their mouths. Halil stood behind me, one hand on my shoulder, the other holding a full coffee pot. "Halil got a wonderful, well, wonderful isn't even big enough to describe it. Halil got this really fabulous job."

"What's the difficult part?" added my father, cracking his knuckles before placing his palms solidly on either side of his plate. Suddenly, I was overwhelmed with the news myself and bowed my head in a feeble attempt to hide the tears that began pouring from my eyes. "Hal, what's going on?" continued my father in an eerie voice, deep and controlled.

Behind me, I felt Halil bristle. He hates his name anglicized. "The job is back home. In Bahrain."

My mother's fork clattered to the floor, Halil moved to relieve himself of the coffee pot, and I looked beseechingly at my parents. "It's a wonderful job. Chief of Staff at the biggest hospital. And I want to go."

"No, no, no, Deborah. You can't. The Middle East? No. I forbid it." She spoke frantically and irrationally. "No. You can't. It's dangerous, a dangerous world. Saddam Hussein lives around there. And the Palestines! They bomb Christians, whole busloads. No."

But I wouldn't be a Christian, Ma.

Halil and I had spent hours role-playing in the previous days, ever since we'd found out. I said, as humbly as I could, though my voice quavered and my throat stung, "You can't forbid it."

"You're my daughter; I most certainly can!" exclaimed my mother.

"I'm twenty-nine years old, living by myself, and going to marry. You *forbid* me? Are you nuts?" Never before had I felt such a bizarre combination of anger, fear, and anguish.

"Only I, as her husband, could do that."

We all stared at Halil.

"So the truth comes out," said my father.

"What? You wouldn't be doing that either!"

Halil took my hands. "It came out wrong. I didn't mean it like that; you know that. I respect and admire your individualism, your Western . . . ism. You know that," he repeated, squeezing my hands to the point of near pain and pleading with his eyes. I interpreted: *Don't embarrass me.*

"Yes, there's your answer," began my mother, finding her voice amid the dark and silent looks around my table. "Already, he's controlling you. Brainwashing you. I dare say he'll be beating you in no time." Halil turned on his heel and left the room. He went into my bedroom where, ironically, he'd only been once before, to bring me tea when I'd caught a summer flu.

"This is out of control, not the way it was supposed to go," I wailed. "And what do you mean, beating? That's ridiculous. Halil's as gentle as a baby. My God, he's got less of a temper than you, Dad!" My mother gasped at this apparently blasphemous statement. My father made fists and pounded the table, making the remnants of my civilized brunch shudder.

"Get your coat, Sofia. We're going." The man I had adored for twenty-nine years pushed himself away from my table and stalked to the door. He stood with his back to us, his hand on the knob. "I will not have you comparing me to some foreigner who only wants my white daughter as a trophy. I will not have it. Not when I am only trying to protect you. If you choose this path, you choose it alone."

I was flabbergasted beyond a response, but my mother had a lucid moment. "David, you don't mean that. We simply can't leave it like this. Please, darling. Be sensible. This is our baby daughter; we love her."

"Sofia Ruth, get your coat and come with me, or move to Baghdad, or wherever the hell he said, with them. You know I mean it." He yanked open the door and was gone. My mother gave me an anguished look and scuttled out after him. The elevator went *ping*. I ran to the bathroom and threw up eggs, coffee, and everything else that was part of me.

Halil stayed in my bedroom with the door shut for an hour. I left him, not sure who was supposed to approach whom, and telephoned my parents' house continuously. My father, I assumed, who'd never gone within six feet of the answering machine, had disconnected it, for I couldn't even leave a message. When Halil finally emerged, his face wore the kind and keen expression I had come to know, but it was tinged with gray. We held each other, perhaps for lack of anything else to do.

"Halil," I said into his warm neck. "What did you mean? What did you mean only you can forbid me?"

He moved his hands and held my face. "I don't know, Deborah. I really don't. I have no desire for any kind of control over you. I'm not like that. It just came out because I was angry at their accusations. You will be my equal partner."

I let out my breath. *I knew it.*

"It's just that in Saudi, people will expect you, us, expect *us* to behave more traditionally. Remember they operate under *sharia*. I guess I was thinking of that."

I'd been earnestly studying the legal system of Saudi Arabia, so very deeply based in religious beliefs, but now I could only quake at his reminder.

That was a September Sunday.

⋆

Two days later, a Saudi exile turned the whole world upside down.

Then on Friday, as I stood in the playground supervising the lunch break shenanigans, I spotted my father approaching. I ran to him with the exuberance of the frolicking children around me, but when I saw his face, I wanted to disappear among the throngs.

He seemed smaller, frailer, than just the previous weekend.

"Daddy."

"You simply cannot go. Now more than ever."

I gaped at him. The emotions of the week had already nearly

debilitated me, and now this? He was crying; my father stood before me, his eyes streaming. I said what my mother had always said to Raquel's and my tears: "If you look up to God, your tears can't fall down."

He ignored me and wiped his eyes, angered at his intimate display. "You cannot go live with those people. Look what they are capable of. They are goddamn monsters."

I swallowed, trying to collect my thoughts. Finally, I replied, "Okay, yes! The terrorists, the extremists, are. But they are not Halil, not Saudi Arabia. They are not what Islam is."

He grabbed my shoulders, started shaking me, and shouted, "You don't believe that!"

"I do!"

I tried to wrench out of his grip, but he held fast. "You stupid, stupid child! Don't do this . . ."

. . . *to yourself? to me?* I didn't know.

Basketballs and jump ropes were stilled as clusters of innocent and confused faces stared at us. Clusters of minds I taught every day to live with tolerance and truth.

I was mortified, devastated, terrified.

The bell rang, and my father did an about-face and left me. A Grade Two student I'd taught the previous year came close and took my hand. I burst into tears and abandoned my playground duties.

I spent October trying to make peace with my parents, but only managed to snatch furtive telephone conversations with my mother. Daniel and Raquel informed me that our father would not allow them to mention my name in his presence. They tried to convince me it was just his way of coping. For their part, my siblings took the news quite well, though my sister told me outright that she didn't think I would go through with it.

"C'mon, Deborah, you're not a risk-taker. You never have been. I know you love the guy—and hey, don't get me wrong, he's drop-dead gorgeous and God knows, I like the rich part—but changing religions and moving to a radically different country for him? That's not the little sister I remember, who freaked out for three weeks when she had to change junior high schools."

The day was crisp and clear, and we were walking the seawall. My nieces were somewhere up ahead with their scooters. "I really wish you people would stop drawing examples from a million years ago to characterize me."

She smirked. "Okay, then, that's not the Deborah I know from two years ago, who only wanted to stay within the resort because downtown Manzanillo scared her."

That fact I couldn't object to, so I only shrugged. "Well, that's what love does, I guess."

"Drives you crazy?" she rebutted, but laughed. "Hey, I said I never wanted kids, but look where loving Jacques got me." Her two grubby cherubs whizzed by us in the opposite direction. "And speaking of makin' babies . . . how's that side of things?"

I sidestepped a Rollerblader. "I wouldn't know."

She clamped onto my right elbow. "What? You wouldn't know? You guys aren't doing it? Holy shit!"

"We're waiting."

"He knows there's not going to be blood on the matrimonial sheets to hang out the window, doesn't he?" asked my sister slyly, cocky at this singular point of ancient culture she'd picked up somewhere.

"Shut up. Of course he does. It's not about our pasts; it's about respecting ourselves now."

"Holy shit," she said again. We tramped on in silence, the

November sun suddenly weaker.

The imminence of Christmas strained Halil's and my relationship, as I fought my instincts to keep my eyes open for gifts, and caught myself humming carols or staring wistfully at the sprouting manger scenes.

"Deborah, I told you at the beginning and I'm telling you now: No one," he sighed heavily, "no one, is forcing you to follow Islam, but if you want to be my wife, you must. My family will not accept you otherwise; they are very, very traditional. God knows, they have just gotten used to the fact that you are a white Canadian. Besides, you told me conversion was no problem, so many months ago. Your exact words, I believe, were, 'It won't be a problem, Halil. To me, it's the spirituality that counts.' Do you remember, *ienee*?" I nodded. His words were verbatim. "But that wasn't at Christmastime, was it?" he added, reading my mind. "Maybe you need to celebrate the Christ's birth one more time. Next year, at home, it will be easier."

At home.

I considered briefly that he was using some kind of reverse psychology; it worked regardless. "No. Thanks. For starters, with whom would I celebrate? Raquel and Daniel will be at my parents', and I'm banned from their house. Second, I did make that commitment to you and I'm not reneging." My voice cracked. "It's just hard right now."

He reached for the portable phone and speed-dialled my parents' number. "Try again, to make contact. You need to be with them, in the spirit of family."

"Merry Christmas," chirped my mother, as she always did when answering the phone for the two weeks before Christmas.

"Hi, Ma. Please don't hang up or pretend it's Mrs. B."

The pause was slight before she replied. "It's okay. Apparently your father is out shopping for my Christmas present with Daniel. You know he'll end up buying Shalimar at Shoppers Drug Mart on the afternoon of the twenty-fourth, but at least he's out prowling around this year. Pity the shopgirls."

Buoyed by this relative plethora of information, I gushed on. "Ma, I need to see you. Please. And understand, it was Halil who dialled your number. It's my last, kind of, Christmas."

"Just a moment, dear, the oven dinged." I imagined I heard a cookie sheet being pulled out of the oven and visualized her buttery shortbread. Or maybe sugar cookies formed with the ancient Santa cutter. She was buying time, as opposed to gifts. Eventually, she came back on the line, if she'd ever left at all. "Anyway, honey, say that again?"

"Ma! I want to see you. And Daddy. Maybe you first. Please, Ma."

Did I hear a scraping sound? The spatula lifting the cookies. "I agree, but it can't be here, because your father has become a near-permanent fixture. And it can't be at your house because . . . because, frankly, I can only lie so much, but I have shopping to do. Meet me in front of Chih Ling's at the mall. Saturday noon. It'll be crazy busy, but there's no other choice."

No other choice to do the last of your shopping or to see me, Ma?

The week between the telephone call and the reunion turned out to be a critical one for Halil and me. Still, it was so good to see her in front of Chih Ling's, flecked with rice and all.

"I'm sorry, Ma. I didn't want to shock you; it's just that I'm practising wearing my *isharb*. I figure if I can wear it as a minority in Vancouver, I can certainly handle it in Bahrain."

I didn't reveal that I felt more like a Russian babushka, or a

Minnesota farm girl, than the wife of a prominent Saudi doctor.

She looked at me in her practical, mom-like manner, and saw through me. "It's not Hallowe'en dress-up, you know, Deborah."

I might have recoiled, but she said it so gently and it was so true that I could only take it as good advice.

I smiled at her. "Do you want to get a different lunch?" The surviving remnants of her lunch looked mangled and sad on her Styrofoam plate.

"Only if you are, " she sniffed, gazing wistfully at a plate of french fries going by.

"Ah, me? No. Thank you. It's Ramadan. I've chosen to fast during daylight hours. It's to honour . . ."

"The poor, the hungry," she finished without rancour.

I could only raise my brows. Obviously, she'd been reading something. "Yes."

"Well, I'll just grab a coffee, shall I? I need the caffeine to shop for Daniel's gift; he's always so difficult to buy for."

By the time she returned, I was all primed up and blurted out, "Ma, we're leaving the country December twenty-ninth 'cause the hospital wants Halil working by the tenth of January."

She cupped her paper cup in both hands. I salivated at the aromatic steam that wafted from its open top. "I don't know what to say, Deborah. That's soon."

Yes. Sooner than anyone expected.

"Can't you join him later? To give yourself more time?"

But then I might not go at all.

I shook my head slowly. "I need to see the family, together. As a Christian." I winced, unable to reconcile my battling faiths. Wasn't I Muslim now? "Please, ask Daddy to let me in the house. An hour, just to see the kids, Daniel, Raquel, you, him, all together."

She had been fiddling with the lid of the cup, but suddenly jerked her head up. "But the wedding! The wedding. I must host my baby girl's wedding," she wailed, completely off topic.

Maybe not.

I gulped. "Halil's sisters are planning it for February nineteenth, in Ar Riyad, his hometown. You can still come. Anyone can come. I mean, it would have been here, if we hadn't had to move, so quickly." I was grateful her face wasn't a contorted mass of anger, tears, or revulsion, but its blank disbelief was far more disconcerting. "And if it's a matter of money . . ." I added stupidly.

"That's not it," she chastised and I bowed my head, supplicant. Indeed, airfare was not the issue. "I'll have to talk to your father," she said simply. I didn't dare ask which bit she meant to discuss. She gave herself a gentle shake, as one would to settle a new hairstyle, and sipped her coffee daintily. "Now, let me tell you what I found for our little Sarah. . . ."

✳

My mother waited, for a million justified reasons I'm sure, until the twenty-third to call me. "I," she said like she was reading from a bad script, "would be overjoyed to welcome you to our home, your home, Christmas Eve." I envisioned Father O'Neil and my mother's best friend, Mrs. B., hovering offstage, mouthing the words. I saw my father hunched over an engine of some sort. I couldn't bring myself to ask why only she would be overjoyed.

"And Halil?" I inquired levelly.

"Oh, yes," flowed my mother, a consummate actress, "I'll be able to squeeze in some mincemeat tarts." Obviously, my father was not far off after all and uttering Halil's name was still forbidden. Ma had two days to work a veritable miracle. At least she hadn't euphemized Halil as a slice of Quebecois pork tortière.

On Christmas Eve, at exactly eight o'clock, my fiancé and I stood at my parents' seasonally wreathed front door. Tucked under Halil's arm was a festive bottle of sparkling apple juice. I balanced a pan of gooey baklava, a debacle of green and pink icing smeared on as a panicked effort to meld two worlds.

Eight people wrapped in smiles worthy of any doctrine greeted us at the door. Though I'd worn my *isharb* unnecessarily—we'd be indoors with family, after all—it dislodged during the embraces, fully exposing my new, raven-coloured hair and eliciting gasps. I'd decided my hazel eyes and apricot skin would stand out enough in a land of chocolately complexions.

"You look like Elizabeth Taylor," chided my brother, and I had to take it as a compliment.

Raquel's husband pressed a gigantic Coke into Halil's hand, my mother kissed him chastely on the cheek, and the others gave us hugs or hearty thumps on the back. My father was nowhere to seen.

"He's next door," whispered Raquel, "at the Steinburgers'. Threw Ma's favourite Royal Doulton, the ballerina, into the fireplace and left."

"And I'm to damn well chalk that up as a mere coping mechanism as well?" I regretted my loss of composure immediately and began to shake.

Raquel gripped my wrists. "Your presence is what Ma wants. You know I think you're nuts, and you'll be back here in a year, but it's your life. Ma votes you'll hang in there. She's seeing this as, like, your final Christmas present to each other. So get your butt into the living room and enjoy."

"But Daddy, what if he never . . ."

"There's nothing more you can say or do until he sees for

himself if you made the right decision. It won't be forever. It just won't." She grinned at me wickedly. "In the meantime, you'll have all those sheiks and sultans and shahs and stuff to play Dada."

I punched her in the arm. "Don't be ignorant."

"Go relax. Want me to slip a little something extra into your apple juice?"

Raquel, as incorrigible as ever. I smiled blandly at her and joined the hubbub in the living room.

We spoke mostly of past Christmases all evening. My brother-in-law Jacques, a total francophone, related his rendition of his first Christmas with us, when Daddy couldn't make heads or tails of his accent. Halil smiled in the right places, but we all registered that French Catholic to Italian Catholic was no comparative stretch. I had half an ear to the porch door; we all did, I'm sure, waiting to hear it slam, and the sound of my father stamping his boots. It didn't happen. It was Daniel who finally showcased my father's retirement project to Halil, the reconstruction of a '58 Chevy.

I escaped into the kitchen and assessed my stark hair in the warped reflection of the toaster. My head scarf hung slack around my neck; it had a mind of its own, going askew every time I moved.

It just didn't feel right.

I mean, I still wasn't folding it right, or perhaps it was the fabric. Halil's sisters would soon instruct me well. This night, when Halil caught me fiddling, he'd gently and unobtrusively reach over and help me make the adjustment, knowing and supporting how important the symbol had become to me.

I was still gawking at myself when my mother bustled in to refill the Santa plate of shortbread. She reminded me for the hundredth time how much butter to use because, she insisted, "Shortbread can be served for any special occasion. That *moolid* one, for instance."

A Saint's Day.

Tears started rolling down my face, and I fled the kitchen to the bathroom. Soon, there would be nowhere to escape from what I was asking myself to become.

When I finally emerged from the john, she corralled me again and pressed a signature turquoise Birk's box into my hand. I figured it'd be a crucifix. It had the size and weight of one, and they were her standard gift every few decades. I was due.

It was a pendant all right, but a plain silver disc, the diameter of a quarter, on which was simply inscribed, "Go with God." She reached out to me and fumbled with the clasp of the gold chain my father had given me on my twenty-first birthday. She dropped my twenty-one-year-old crucifix—I hadn't yet been able to remove it—into her palm, threaded the chain with her gift, and re-hung it around my neck. Her hug surged with emotion, as did mine.

Daddy had still not come home. Family history suggested he would come around eventually, as Raquel had assured, but this was so incredibly different than debating worthy university majors or fighting over insipid fashion trends. I wondered if I should pray for his acceptance, or the strength to follow my new convictions with no further comment.

So I didn't pray at all.

When my mother and I returned to the living room, my *isharb* again in disarray from our embrace, Raquel studied us, then pulled two bobby pins out of her chic French twist. She moved her gaze to my soon-lover, my on-earth Islamic mentor, my answer to indecisiveness, then handed one pin to my mother, the other to Halil.

In tandem, they secured the soft white muslin.

Piggy Paula

Piggy Paula Fisher lumbered home from Frieda Scholer Elementary School via the Frontage Road. Half of her mind was consumed with hopes that the four o'clock *Brady Bunch* wouldn't be a rerun; the other half connected with her fingers as they desperately searched her Shaun Cassidy knapsack for change to use at the Rolling Sage Motel vending machine.

So named by her classmates, and some adults alike, Piggy Paula dared herself to say out loud, "There must be another f'ing nickel in here somewhere." For Piggy Paula, this was quite a statement, audience or not.

She was so focused on finding change, it was a near miracle she didn't get hit by a car, a motorcyclist, or even another pedestrian. The closer she got to the motel, the less important the antics of Jan, Marsha, Bobby, and the rest of the perfect, integrated Brady clan became and the more important finding a means to a quick fix grew.

Piggy Paula couldn't find the necessary nickel for even cheap mints, but made the slight detour to the machines anyway, in case some tourist from Calgary or Seattle happened to have left change in the little slot. She wiggled three bloated fingers up its metal vagina, to no avail. Irritated because it was her mother's short day at work and that made a satisfactory forage of the cupboards difficult, Piggy Paula continued home, hustling as much as she was capable of through the graffiti-swirled highway underpass.

Brad loves Cindy. suck my dick royally. Jesus saves.

She wondered how a dick was sucked royally and how a Jesus-freak could ignore the damage to property law in order to send a message. She pet the ancient collie chained to Mr. Dobson's front porch, pondering if her mother had taken the leftover fried chicken to work for lunch.

Piggy Paula was eleven years old, four-foot-ten, and 147 pounds, perhaps a titch more. No one said things like, "But she's got such a pretty face," because frankly, she did not. It was usually streaked with something: a smoosh of chocolate, a daub of jam, a crusting of tomato sauce. Her eyes were embedded marbles of wishy-washy hazel that shot this way and that, never settling on anything long enough to give a suggestion of approachability. In fact, people avoided speaking to Piggy Paula at all.

Mrs. Fisher was on her knees, ridding the front garden of spiky grass, when Piggy Paula entered the yard. Her mother was obsessed with that garden, truly. No one else on the street, in mid-October, was still furiously stirring and mixing, patting and scooping their gardens like Mrs. Fisher. The ground looked like mounds of chocolate shavings.

Please God, please God, please: Have her stay outside for a while longer.

"Hi, Mom."

"Hello, honey. How was your day?" Mrs. Fisher rocked back on her heels and peered at her daughter. Paula had long ago decided that her mother looked just like the stick women in the cave paintings they'd studied in Social Studies.

She squirmed under her mother's assessment, and tugged at the knees of her Round Gal jeans. They grazed her ankle bones, and she knew her mother was thinking about putting an extension on them. Last time, it'd been a ruffle of purple gingham and the resulting taunts at school had been much worse than the regular, "Flood's over, flood's over."

Piggy Paula shrugged in response to her mother's daily question, as automatic as the new dishwasher. "Don't forget I'm babysitting George the Gerbil next weekend. I got lots of homework. I'm gonna do it right now, so I can watch *Little House* tonight."

"Going to. Not gonna. No snacking, dear," instructed Mrs. Fisher, turning back to immerse herself in the dirt. Elsie Fisher was an *immersed* kind of woman.

Inside, Piggy Paula moved in her own efficient ballet. After tossing her school bag onto her bed, she stopped to lock the back door to impede her mother's approach—Mrs. Fisher would never use the front door after gardening. She surveyed the pantry (the creaky door made secret missions nearly impossible) before removing a box of Triscuits and two tins of smoked oysters she'd shoved to the very back of the cupboard while helping unload groceries. From the refrigerator, Piggy Paula plucked half a package of processed cheese slices, lamenting that there was no more of the funky squeezy cow-teat kind. She snapped off a coil of pepperoni as long as she knew a penis to be and seconded the Tupperware container of chicken—two juicy thighs and a wing. Finally, gripping a carton of orange juice in her teeth, she kicked shut the fridge and pantry doors and shuffled down the hall.

Paula's bedroom door did not lock. Her parents' room did, as well as the bathroom, if only for their guests' peace of mind. She could only buy moments of private time by jamming her desk chair under the knob, an infrequent rebellion that always cost her a week without TV.

"What could you possibly have to hide?" her mother had retorted last June, when Piggy Paula broached the subject of a lock. "You're eleven."

"Shayla Williams has a lock on her door *and* her own bathroom."

Mrs. Fisher was concentrating on a TV cooking show and seemed tired of the conversation already. She waved her daughter away with a long, bony hand. "We have no secrets in this house," she'd informed Paula. "Go outside and play."

After slipping two cheese rolls from the baking canister into the pocket of her Big Gal's denim jumper and retrieving the hidden remainder of black licorice, provided by her father, she had wandered outside.

She could think of nothing to do. The Skookum River behind the house was running too high to explore, and Paula knew she looked like a Shrine circus clown riding her teeny bicycle up and down the driveway. Her boredom was relentless, for although she could imagine foods of infinite textures and tastes and create luscious delicacies in her mind out of both living and inanimate objects, she had little imagination beyond that.

She'd decided to go next door and tap on Gabbi Varvarinski's bedroom window with several strands of licorice.

But she'd seen light squeezing out from the closet and knew it would be useless to hang around. Gabbi Varvarinski could stay in that closet reading her stupid books for hours; Piggy Paula had tried to wait it out several times. Gabbi's mom was locked away in a nuthouse; everybody knew. Sometimes Paula thought about a nuthouse for fat people and wondered if her mother would send her there.

She'd left two whips on the windowsill, a calling card of sorts, and plodded back home to see if her mother would now allow her a snack, given that she'd occupied herself outside for a total of nine minutes.

Now, four months later on a cool October afternoon, the craving to chew and swallow, chew and swallow was reaching a fever pitch, calling to Piggy Paula like heroin to a junkie. Her jaw was slack, her tongue floating in saliva; she felt like a dog watching its dish being filled. Piggy Paula placed her schoolbooks on her bed in a semicircle, to suggest she was a studious girl with several important projects on the go. The goodies, however, went under the bed in a neat row, hidden by the fringe of the chenille bedspread. She lay perpendicular to the bed, the newly vacuumed, mustard-coloured shag carpet flattening beneath her, and erected thirteen wobbly silos of cheese, crackers, gouged-off hunks of pepperoni, and squiggly smoked oysters. Only when the towers were perfectly arranged did she begin thrusting them between quivering lips.

Piggy Paula had always been fat. It was one of those things, just as her father had always worked at the mill, and the river had always flowed behind their house. She was six or seven when the kids at school picked up the Piggy Paula bit: "Paula, Paula, two by four, couldn't fit through the bathroom door, so had to do it, on the floor." It practically became the school anthem.

The trouble was, eating was solving nothing. Gobbling packet after packet, container after container, trying to eat enough to turn inside out—or simply explode—did not stop his hunger.

At dinner that night, she waited tensely as always, sometimes with cause, sometimes not, for her mother to mention the missing chicken (or block of cheese, or tub of ice cream, or leftover noodles).

Paula watched her father tuck the paper serviette into his collar and crack his knuckles in preparation to eat. He would ritually cut his meat into bite-sized pieces, sigh and pat his compact belly when finished.

However, through tonight's Shake 'n Bake chops, mashed potatoes, and julienned carrots, Mrs. Fisher reported only wallpapering plans.

"Daddy, can we get a puppy?" asked Paula when Mrs. Fisher paused.

"No. The answer is still no."

"A kitty?"

Instead of answering, her father eyed her plate with palatable distaste. "You don't need another pork chop," he growled. "My Christ, you eat more than me. Elsie, put this girl on a diet."

Elsie Fisher was in the middle of describing the hues she envisioned for the back bedroom. "Frank, you interrupted. You know I hate that. Besides, I've put her on many diets, but she's a sneaker. A food sneaker," she emphasized. "It's not my fault."

Piggy Paula pressed two chunks of chop into her mouth, lest it get taken away, before exclaiming, "Mother! I don't sneak anything." A piece of half-chewed meat fell out of her mouth and plopped onto the table.

"That's goddamn disgusting," growled Frank Fisher.

"Don't talk with food in your mouth, Paula," instructed Mrs. Fisher automatically. "And don't start with each other, you two.

Paula, honey, that's enough. Drink some water if you're still hungry. Frank, we need to support, not tease or threaten."

"Support?" he barked, rising from the table. "The floorboards aren't gonna support her if she keeps on this way."

"What about the bedsprings, Daddy?" inquired Piggy Paula, daring only a fleeting look at him. She felt a drop of grease roll down her chin.

Paula's heart thudded under the gaze of his huge, sunken eyes. They narrowed and widened, narrowed and widened with indecision as to how he would respond. Finally, slowly, he released the tiniest of smiles at her before scrunching his serviette. He dropped the wad onto his plate and said tightly, "I'm going to my meeting. I'll be home around ten."

His Elks' meeting, held the third Tuesday of each month. Paula felt both relieved and wary. She was supposed to be asleep by ten on a school night, though he usually woke her, sometimes by poking her with a chocolate bar.

Once the Dodge had backed out of the driveway, Mrs. Fisher said, "Honey, you really are getting to be a big girl. Don't you want to cut down a little? It would mean a lot to your father."

"I'll do the dishes, Mom."

"He means well, your father."

Piggy Paula felt the contents of her stomach shift. Making room for more. "You can go watch TV."

"He loves you, you know. Your father loves you."

"And that's all that counts," whispered Paula, willing her mind to carry her to a land of taco chips and pumpkin pie, macaroni and cheese eaten out of the pot with the same wooden spoon that had once tanned her behind. She scraped her parents' plates, stacked them, and moved everything into the kitchen.

And your kind of love? What kind is that? You're so stupid, Mother. You didn't even notice the chicken was gone. You'll never remember about the oysters. You're just so stupid in your doctor's-receptionist-gardening-little-world.

Elsie Fisher leaned against the doorframe. "Paula, it's not my fault, you know."

"I don't want to talk about it, Mother. About being fat."

Her mother sighed and padded off down the hallway to catch the last of the CBC news hour; Paula paused a second before slurping back the flaccid bits of pork fat she'd scraped onto the top plate. She used a finger to clean the mashed potato pot to a near gleam, but happily threw out the last spoonful of carrot. When she was done loading the dishes and handwashing those which had been banned from automation, Paula took out the bulging kitchen garbage, stealthily stopping at her room to add the cheese wrappings, metal oyster tins, and empty Triscuits box to the bag.

At nine, Elsie Fisher announced she had a migraine; she usually did on Tuesday nights. Apparently her medication was a very powerful sedative. Before retiring, she gave her daughter a kiss on top of her head and cautioned her against raiding the refrigerator. She would have been barely settled amid the matching pillows and duvet before Paula found herself back in the middle of the kitchen, debating which cupboard would yield the best harvest.

She chose the cupboard above the stove and was gratified to see that her mother had silently replaced the box of Wagon Wheels surreptitiously polished off in previous days. She stashed the marshmallow and chocolate disks for later and took the rest of the processed cheese slices to nibble during *Dynasty*.

The ninth plastic cheese casing was lying in her lap when the headlights of the blue Dodge dragged across the entire living room like a Hollywood spotlight as Frank Fisher exacted his parking. The beams swooped across the mantle, resplendent with family portraits. There was one of Paula, fresh home from the hospital where, ironically, she'd started life in an incubator. Next to it was chubby six-year-old Paula, taking her first communion. She remembered wishing the priest would hurry, so the cake and ice cream party could begin.

But getting fat was not enough to keep him away; it only meant her mother resorted to headshots only, as if the burgeoning body beyond the frame did not exist.

Paula crumpled the cheese wrappings and stuffed them deep into the cushion of the recliner, wondering whether to stay up or feign sleep. As Frank Fisher turned his key in the lock, Paula bustled to retrieve her Grade Six reader. Sometimes she could put him off by claiming homework.

"How's my girl?" greeted Frank Fisher, leaning over the back of the La-Z-Boy, where she'd awkwardly pretzelled herself.

He dropped an Oh Henry! bar into the open spine of the reader. "I'm sorry I gave you a tough time at dinner, honey."

Piggy Paula tried to focus on the farmer lady in the story who had to sell her tea set to buy grain. "That's okay, Daddy." He'd stopped off for a drink or two after the meeting; she could smell it. "I need to finish this story. We're having a quiz on it, first thing tomorrow." She left the chocolate bar where it had landed and continued staring at the reader until the words swirled together like butterscotch in ice cream.

"Okay. We'll be quick. C'mon, Paula. Come do Daddy a favour, then you can study and eat your bar."

"I can't, Daddy. I really have to finish this."

"Paula," said Frank Fisher evenly, still leaning over the thick arm of the chair and speaking to the back of her head. "Paula, you owe me, remember? You promised 'next time' if I let you watch that goddammed pioneer show. Remember?" His hand, warm and rough, reached around and massaged the swollen wattle of flesh at her throat. "Remember?"

"Yes," she whispered.

"Well, okay then." His voice, the message behind the words, was like a lemon sour candy: the first tonguing deceptively sweet, biting into it a wicked jolt of tang.

He gently took Paula's hand and led her to her own bedroom, where she robotically removed her clothes and then his scratchy navy dress pants.

Her bedside lamp was on and she knew if she looked down, she'd see it. Sometimes, strangely, it made her giggle. Tonight she thought she might cry and he got mad at that, so she focused on her doll collection.

He slapped at her bare, protruding belly playfully at first, as one might test a watermelon for ripeness, then squeezed more forcefully, as if he were molding playdough. Frank Fisher tugged at the little tuft of wiry hair starting to form between her legs and grunted his disapproval.

"Jesus H. Christ, girl," he said softly as he moved his hand around to caress her buttocks. "You've got the body of a forty-year-old Negroid woman."

She didn't know what that meant, didn't know how to take such a description.

She imagined his whiskey breath to be chocolate-flavoured while waiting for his controlled whinny and, as a precaution against her imminent fertility, the spurt of cum onto her stomach.

Like the drippings of a Dairy Queen vanilla shake.

In moments, he was up and fetching a wet towel. He even brought the chocolate bar and reader from the living room.

"Sleep tight, Paula. Do your teeth when you finish your treat."

The wrapper was already off the bar by the time he'd closed her door.

The Wagon Wheels waited silently under the bed.

Twenty-Eight Days

Tisha awakes with the heavy, thick head that comes from drinking red wine by day and chasing it with an afternoon nap on a futon ablaze with syrupy September sun. She oozes her way into the bathroom and lies down on the tiles, seeking the shock of the cold, hard ceramic, but also the excuse to lie down again.

It's a tiny, apartment-sized bathroom and she lies crosswise, her head squished between the tub and the toilet, one leg behind the door, the other spilling into the hallway. She lies, a starfish of sorts, and feels the coldness of the tiles penetrate her backside, like a reverse barbeque. Her eyes flutter open and shut, so the state of her bathroom is captured in the style of a slide show. Two dead flies in the light covering. Fade to black. A crusty yellow drizzle of something down the outside of the toilet bowl. Fade to black. A colourful stack of rolled towels running up the wall, reminding her of a roll of assorted LifeSavers. Fade to black.

When the cold of the tiles penetrates halfway, say, from her shoulder blades to the base of her floppy boobs and up through the small of her back to where she imagines her uterus to be anchored, she flips over.

Now Tisha lies like a chalked-out corpse: her right knee drawn up, her right cheek pressed into the cross of four tiles meeting, her hands over her head as if she was pantomiming a halo when struck down. She feels the grit of the floor on her face and palms and spies a lost lipstick lying in the corner, just beside the plunger.

After a time—it may have been one minute, it may have been thirty—she draws herself up, using the edge of the tub, the towel rack, the counter. She peers into the mirror, her only light the milky spillover from the hallway. The mirror, speckled with backwash from splashing in the sink, excess hairspray, and talc, skews her reflection. Slightly. Not enough to be anyone but herself. Not enough to not recognize herself. She tugs at the spirals of blonde hair, purses thin lips, slaps a rather bulbous stomach. *If it sticks out now. . . .*

She wonders when he'll be back.

The little round disc lies on top of the Tupperware container of cosmetics. New, full, complete. She flips it over so the twenty-one little pink eyes will not be able to stare at her and is disappointed to see that there is no winning answer embossed on the back.

Sam is out somewhere, being paternal with the dog. The dog had been promised snow, a play in the mountain snow, like a child might be promised a visit to Pizza Hut. She imagines them romping around Mount Seymour, Sam trying to convince Au Lait to retrieve tennis balls when all the dog ever wants to do is run around in circles and mark the snow.

Tisha is forced into full alertness by the knock-knock-knock. It's her next-door neighbour, returning the job section of the Saturday newspaper. Plus, she holds up a purchase for Tisha's inspection: a two-hundred-dollar pair of thigh-high red leather boots.

"Aren't they cool?" gushes the neighbour, whose name is something cute that ends in *i*. Judi/Barbi/Bambi seems unaware of the incongruence of holding both the expensive boots and the rumpled section of Person Friday positions.

"They are cool," agrees Tisha, fingering the proffered leather. Silky as a baby's bottom.

"I'm wearing them to the Commodore tonight. I'm, like, totally psyched." *i*-girl cradles the boots as she backs away. "Well, thanks for the paper. Again. There was a coupla good ones."

"Yes. Good luck," says Tisha and closes the door as quickly as possible. The fight with Sam, with *time*, has left her feeling unsociable, especially towards nubile nymphs.

An apparition of *i*-girl's red, thigh-high leather boots follows Tisha all day, clunking after her when she grocery shops, daring her to buy things like 47 per cent milk-fat foreign cheese, and fresh prawns the size of her thumb. They dare her into decadence.

The damn things sidle up to her outside Le Chateau as well— a shop she has not been in for years, since her twenties—and tap impatiently as she studies frivolous jackets, slippy baby tees, microminis in silver Spandex. In the warped, smoked-glass mirror, Tisha mentally dresses a holograph image of herself in outfit after outfit.

The black vinyl biker dress, with its chunky zippers that *whoosh!* transform it into a shirt and *shazam!* into a vest, is not even on sale. She buys it on Visa because it is so many things, not just one boring thing; she buys it because it is not a clearly identifiable, pigeonholed garment in washable cotton, but a layer of secrets and diversity that no one expects.

No expectations. That's good.

Back at home, she finds Sam sitting on the couch, his reading glasses on, studying the financial section with the same baffled intensity as she had studied the kumquats, the push-up bras, and the new Spring line of fuck-me heels in cobalt and ecru. Au Lait, the beige mutt from the SPCA, lies on his back beside Sam, proudly displaying what's left of his genitals.

"Hi," she says, tentatively. The first, post-blowout verbal connection is always the weirdest, the riskiest.

He looks up and smiles tiredly. "Hi, babe. Where ya been?"

She shrugs, shielding the Le Chateau sack and Urban Fare grocery bag. "A little shopping."

"A little thinking?" Sam suggests. His voice is neutral, but his words carry enough voltage that she drops the love-food. The seven-dollar jar of pickled partridge eggs smashes open when it hits the ceramic tiles; rubbery ovums bounce in all directions. Au Lait is off the couch and gulping them down before Tisha can shove him away and angrily toss the remainder into the garburator. She cuts herself cleaning up the glass and recoils at the blood.

Sam, though he looks on with concern, stays seated. Having shot out his unwelcome query, apparently his participation is done.

"Don't start," she warns. She snatches up the food bag and tosses it into the fridge, like it's a mere gunnysack of potatoes. Anger always makes her tongue flippant and her actions reckless.

To escape, to avoid the millions of little questioning beams he emits, Tisha pours a fresh glass of wine, goes into the bedroom, and shuts the door—a 98 per cent safe barrier-method—to his output. She stretches out on the bed with a pad of foolscap and the pen Au Lait once used as a pacifier, though she is not sure what she wishes to create.

She tries a Pros and Cons list, but both columns remain empty. (*Ergo*, the problem.) She tries adding up the cost factor, but finds she has no idea what such things are worth financially or otherwise.

She doodles the initials of old boyfriends, men that would take her side for certain. She wouldn't have to flip, or flip out. She considers calling them for support, for old times' sake, for her ego. To force everyone's hands. Actually, it would be a sneaky diversion, to make crises where none exist. The old smoke-and-mirrors trick.

He'd said in the morning, before storming out with the dog, "You promised!"

"I did no such thing," she'd shot back. *I wouldn't be so stupid.*

That shut him up, because he knew it was true. But had she ever actually said "no," either? As in, "Just Say No?" Unlikely, because she'd never meant no. Or yes. Nice. Nice climax to eight years of natal nonchalance.

Eventually, Tisha returns to the living room and stands in front of the Canucks, who are losing. He mutes the TV and looks at her inquiringly; she knows she doesn't have long. If he leans to the left to catch the replay of some slapshot, she will lose her nerve. (The truth is, she hopes he does move to the side, show distraction, impatience. Then she can have a grand temper tantrum, the source of which will become so convoluted, the real issue will no longer matter.)

"The question is, for me, 'Do I want this marriage and your happiness enough to do something that may or may not make me happy?' Your question is, 'Do you want a baby badly enough that you would leave this marriage if I don't say yes?'"

Was that a tilt of his head?

"Are you looking at the TV? Because if you are . . ."

"I'm not!" Sam assures her, being careful to first look at her, then pull her into his lap and pivot away from the screen, as his own insurance policy, Tisha suspects. "I'm thinking. Those are harsh questions."

"They're the crux of it, aren't they? How bad do we each want what we want?"

"Or think we want."

"*Touché*. Or want each other."

They sit, entwined in silence, the comfortable posturing something she loves about marriage. She watches the countdown clock in the upper corner of the screen. The Canucks and Bruins are into overtime.

"I need more time," Tisha says.

"But I don't want to be throwing a ball with my kid when I'm fifty years old."

She groans. This is his stock response. She swallows a testy rebuttal. "Let me be honest and give you another scenario. I don't know if it's some kind of threat to myself or you or what, but a fear of yours should be that if you give me another year and I still don't know, or say no, you'll have lost another year for nothing."

Suddenly, Tisha feels irritated. *Why am I pointing out this shit to him? He should be thinking out his own questions and have the guts to ask them.*

But she knows she is the problem-maker of the two, the thinker, the obsessor—that without her ambivalent probing, they would go on indefinitely with her batting away Sam's glib "let's make a baby" comments, as if they were harmless but irksome houseflies. Until the feelings build up in him again, like this morning, when his frustration and yearning spawned angry barbs and threats. She wouldn't tell him she preferred rage over gentle chiding because then at least one of them was exhibiting passion.

Tisha peels herself off his lap, pours herself the last of the wine, and leaves him to the hockey game. She wanders into the bathroom. The tiny, apartment-sized bathroom.

Picking up the disk of Ortho 7/7/7, she flicks off the teeny cover for the first Sunday and tongues the pill into her mouth, feeling neutralized, relieved, and sad, all at once. She swallows the baby-stopper and thinks that perhaps in another twenty-eight days, the gods will see fit to finally intervene and make the decision for them. For her.

She thinks about the red leather thigh-highs, the biker dress. She'll go put it on and make peace when the game's finished. Overtime can't last forever.

Little Messes

I would have preferred the screen door to slam behind me, for effect, you know? Instead, it fell clear off and went *splat* on the porch, as it's been threatening to do for years now. It was something, but not the same as slamming. Then Germ, who—or *to whom*, I know there's a rule, but I'll be damned if I remember it—the slam was directed, could concentrate on the flattened door instead of the fighting words I'd just thrown. At him.

My galootish, missing-nothing-in-the-body-department boyfriend has always had weird good timing like that, and it makes me woof my cookies. Like the time he left the outhouse with the tin roof, still hitching up his ugly GWGs, right before it got hit by lightning and split in two.

"Like the crack of an arse," Germ'd commented calmly.

"Like a cleaver coming down on a melon," had been my observation; try as I might, I can't match Germ's crudeness.

Or there was the time he'd just left Spider Dirk's Junkyard in Ashcroft, and the Mounties came and did a big raid on Spider's backroom moonshine operation. Spider, his girlfriend, and some old fart looking for '59 Thunderbird hubcaps all got arrested.

"'Bout time the fuzz broke that up," I'd said when Germ gave me the report. I was busy taping plastic over the kitchen window to help cut Sage's bitter winter draft. "He sells to minors and somebody's going to end up blind."

"It wasn't hurting anybody," replied Germ, ever the diplomat. "Didn't hear you complaining when he gave you that jug for your birthday."

I shimmied my brain back in time. "No. He didn't give me a damn thing, even after all those sandwiches he's scoffed down in my kitchen because he always arrives to see you right at lunch."

Germ had suddenly looked real sheepish and I got the picture. "Why, you two little pisstanks! You drank it, didn't you? What a couple of . . ." then I stopped. Germ's grin had turned Cheshire cat, and I knew it'd be no use to continue.

My friend Bri said Germ's got a golden horseshoe up his wazoo. I told her obviously not far enough, or we wouldn't live in Mr. McEachern's summer cottage all year long just 'cause we keep the juvie-Ds from breaking in and using his cutlery for hot-knifing. We live down a long lane, off a normal street full of normal houses. None of the kids come trick-or-treating because the lane's too scary at night and also probably because their mamas tell them to stay away from the hippie house. It's my long cotton dresses and Germ's Grizzly Adams beard that do it. They probably think I'd lace my goodies with pot or acid. I wouldn't. First, because I don't think that stuff's for kids, and second, I just wouldn't waste it on the little buggers. Anyway, the cottage is left over from when this

area of Sage was the boonies, but it's grown so much, we're practically part of a regular suburb now.

My real name's Louisa May, but from way back folks've called
me Wizzy. I was twenty-five years old last March-ish. I say "ish"
'cause my birthday's on the ninth, but my mom's present didn't
arrive from Regina 'til the twelfth and Germ didn't remember 'til
he watched me folding the brown paper she'd wrapped the herb
book in. On the fifteenth. Then he got all sucky and mumbled on
and on about not finishing the present he was still working on in
the garage.

We both know that was cow-tooties 'cause Germ knows all he
has to do is hit the Shopper's Drug Mart bath salts section and I'd
be happier than an unhooked Sage Lake trout. Any section, really,
except for toilet paper or tampons; they're about the only two
things I regularly scrounge up enough money to buy. Hell, he
could visit the deodorant section for all I care because nice, minty
or lemony brand-name juice would beat out the no-name bloc-
o-anti-sweat I currently rub on every second day. A coupon laid
out nice on my pillow for cleaning up his crap in the shed, that'd
be nice too.

Hell, I'd take anything that wasn't greasy, old, or brown. I make
ends meet by working days in a local diner dressed in beige polyester, on the weekends in the Pet Rock-sized Sage Museum in a
taupe vest and wraparound skirt, and the odd night at the Juicy
Burger in a tan apron and matching tam. Germ says I'm a walking
advertisement for Uniforms Inc., The Bland Department. Good
thing my hair's strawberry blonde and is an outfit in itself.

Anyway, back to yesterday. After we both stared at the flattened
door for a second or so and I saw that Germ's interest was more
with that dang door than me, I headed out back.

The back garden is only slightly less tame than the front garden. I try to keep the veggies and the marijuana out of the front. Sometimes there's a mother of a squash, and I just let 'er rip, but I usually cut things off at the electric meter on the east and the oak tree on the west, so visitors know we aren't totally uncouth. Germ can tell you the different grades of iron ore by just feeling them, but not the difference between a fiver and a fifty, or a daisy and carrot green.

Ask him why and he'll say it's because he's an artist. "An art*eeste*," he'll say.

"You're an out-of-work, lazy, motherf'ing welder," I screamed at the crux of one particularly hot fight. I was in brown uniform number two and fixing to change into number three. It wasn't a day to be messing with me.

"I'm *avant garde*."

"You don't even know what that means! Or *carpe diem, soufflé, eau de toilet* or anything else except doobies, butt-crack jokes, and soldering tools. Nobody in this whole friggin' town knows anything but mile-high meringue pie, rusting deck chairs on crooked porches, chili cook-offs and . . . and banging out more little snot-noses so the whole damn thing will carry on."

"We have a Mayor, you know," he reminded, whipping his left index finger around the inside of the Spaghettio can for the last of the little pasta wormies. "He knows a lot."

"He knows shit. He got elected 'cause he threatened to spill everybody's sex secrets and if they didn't have any, he bribed them with phony Kmart gift certificates. He knows *nada*."

Oh, we're flaming multilingual in this house.

Anyway, that was another time and another fight about this dumb-ass town, my dumb-ass life.

The one yesterday started while I was up on the wobbly red barstool, watering the zebra plant in the macramé hanger. We were talking money, and Germ was acting all lackadaisical about our financial situation, so I over-watered on purpose. Muddy water splashed onto his upturned, boyish face.

"Well," he said eventually, after realizing it wasn't an accident, or a joke in the ha-ha kind of way. "What is it you see in me and my lazy, ex-welding self then, Wizzy? Why don't you just go back to your crazy Ma or your sisters or Mrs. Baldwin's boarding house?"

I liked towering above him on the stool, no small feat, and willed away the anti-heights thing I had developed ever since sliding off Mr. Carswell's roof when I tried to be neighbourly and coach down his devil-cat, way back in seventh grade. I sure didn't want to say anything complimentary to Germ, like that I stayed because when he touched me my insides felt like hot wax. "I can't up and leave because it's my name on the papers."

"What papers?" he asked suspiciously, suddenly all self-conscious, wiping a gravy-like dribble from his temple. Anything more than rolling papers makes Germ nervous.

I smirked. When you're me, you don't get a chance to smirk too often. Just in case he missed it, I climbed down from my stool and pointed at my face. "See this, Germ? This's a smirk. Means I know better than you. Means I know Mr. McEachern got me to sign a lease because he's smart. No idiot's going to give a house for free." When I'd signed at the bottom of the handwritten page about responsibly using the outhouse and matches and *bearing sole responsibility for the property's occupants*, I thought it was a crock. But it didn't cost me nothing, *any*thing, I mean, to promise to maintain the existing décor and dignity of the place, such as it was, so what the hell.

"Really?" he said, backing away. "Really? Of all the sneaky, bureaucratic, sneaky —"

"You said that."

"—*snakey*, sneaky kinds of things." Then it dawned on him that it meant he was, once again, free of responsibility, and he flashed his cockeyed grin. I liked it when it clouded over again. "So you're like my old lady and my landlady?"

I narrowed my eyes at him, wishing I could hiss and spit like a cobra. After a too-short standoff, I went out for a walk and left it up to him to figure out what it meant.

That's when I met Mrs. Julia, the woman who changed my life forever.

I called her Mrs. Julia for the longest time in my head, but Julia to her face, because I didn't catch her last name when she introduced herself and she seemed like the type that would expect you to catch it on the first go-round.

She'd moved in next door the week before. Her arrival instantly transformed the place, which I assumed was already quite the pad, into a palace-in-waiting. Vans full of burly workers paraded in and out carrying rolls of carpet, huge cardboard boxes, and various other reno-paraphernalia. From the activity, you'd think her house was the Frontage Road convenience store. I openly watched all of this from the end of our drive when I picked up the mail. Okay, and I snuck a few peeks through the dividing hedge, the bit the JWs and Fullerbrush Man cut through.

Fate jumped in and gave me an excuse to venture over.

"Uh, ma'am? I think this is your cat. I guess he's a little freaked out by the drilling and whatnot. He's been hanging out on my porch, in case you've been looking for him. No sweat or anything, but you know, in case you've been looking for him." I was hoping this'd turn out better than my Grade Seven feline rescue and not leave me with any phobias.

"Oh, da Vinci," she crooned, taking him from my awkward arms. "Did da big bad worker men scare da bitty kitty?"

I winced. My grammar wasn't all that good—still isn't—but man, I hate baby-talk. "Anyway, I'm . . ." I stopped. Something about her cool gaze and her perfect, her *impeccable,* apricot-coloured pantsuit kept me from telling her that my name was Wizzy. Louisa May didn't sound right either, considering the last time anybody'd uttered it had been the day I got christened. So I repeated, "Anyway, I'm . . . hungry, so I should go."

If she thought this anything else but a natural response to give a stranger, her face certainly didn't reveal it. Hey, that's classy, I thought.

"Me too. Famished! I have pâté, brie, and chilled Chardonnay. Please join me; if I eat alone, I'll only binge. On the wine, at least," she added conspiratorially.

I'd left Germ with terse instructions to make peanut butter sandwiches, which he'd probably abandoned to melt some down some metal anyway, so I gave a right goofy curtsy and said, "Well, that would be fine."

"And I'm Julia *blahdeblahde*vich," she introduced. "Of course, call me Julia."

As I shook that long cool hand, I realized its only weight came from the gargantuous ruby ring adorning her middle finger. I'd like to flip someone the bird wearing that ring.

"Lovely to meet you, J-j-j-j-julia. I'm Louise."

That afternoon was one of the most amazing of my whole life. Mrs. Julia was a great, a *consummate,* hostess, as far as I could tell in my limited knowledge of afternoon soirees. My wineglass was never empty, and it was sure nice to eat cheese that didn't come in a glass jar or squeeze pack. Though I didn't think I'd like hearing exactly what pâté was, it sure tasted good smeared on teensy moons of French bread.

She asked me a lot about the town, and I gladly filled her in on things like who to avoid, which butcher was a rip-off, and that Sage Road was actually one-way, east to west, even though there were no signs posted since Robbie Cameron took them out with his snowmobile last winter.

"So, are you married?" she asked, tipping the last of the wine into my glass.

"Living in sin. For the last two years."

"Ah. Perhaps that's wise. Divorces are messy and expensive." Just then, a beefy guy stuck his head into the solarium. "Yes, Tony?"

Tony glanced at me quizzically, obviously wondering how I fit into the picture. "Juli . . . uh, Ma'am, I was just wonderin' what time yous wanted to meet to talk about the underlay, for the master bedroom?" Tony was trying real hard to appear nonchalant, but his lust for his employer was so freakin' obvious. So *tangible*.

Julia, however, was smooth. "Perhaps at three o'clock, Tony. I am quite enjoying the company of my new neighbour."

Who, me?

Tony reversed himself out of the doorway.

"Now, where were we?"

"Can I . . . *may* I tell you something?" I whispered. She answered with a slight tilt of her head. "You know that Tony guy has the total hots for you, don't you?"

The tiniest of smiles appeared at the corner of her mouth, like a thin silk thread was attached to the corners and being tugged, ever so slightly.

Finally, she leaned into me. "Don't you think he's delicious? I think of him as a tube of capicollo, solid and spicy."

Her eyes actually glittered, and I shivered in the warm, heady air of the solarium.

When I got home at three, Germ was attaching things to the TV antenna. He goes through this phase every so often, perpetually looking for the ultimate in reception. The town was due for cablevision hookup, not that we'd be able to afford it anyway. He was shirtless and I sure knew what his Levis covered. I got that familiar, good kind of punched-in-the-gut feeling, then the hot wax thing. Tony'd have nothing on my Germ.

I surveyed his latest attempt to de-fuzz Lloyd Robertson. "Germ, those are the only good earrings I have. I don't want to have to come looking for them in the living room. Besides, these mobiles of yours never work."

"You never know."

"I've been at our new neighbour's," I said, a tad petulantly, since it appeared he wasn't going to ask. "Her name is Juuuuuuuulia, and she's maaaaaarvellous. Totally rich, and cultured, and smart, and polite, and beautiful. And, she likes me."

"'Course she does," said Germ distractedly. I sighed and went to get ready for the Juicy Burger. Serving up fountain Coke and limp fries was not exactly a cap on my day.

The next time I toted da Vinci home, Julia answered the door in a long, silver, pearl-beaded gown. I thought it was a bit much for a Sunday morning, even if she was rich.

"Louise!" she greeted, actually clapping her hands in delight. "Just what I need, another woman's opinion. Come in; I'm trying on dresses for a function and I just can't decide. Come in, come in, come in."

Up the winding staircase we went, me feeling like Maria on her first tour of the von Trapp mansion. Julia's king-size bed was frothed with gowns of every colour. It was like looking into a kaleidoscope. I squeaked out a tiny *wow* and tried not to catch my reflection in the giant mirror across the room.

"Now, I adore this one, but the people at the gala, they've seen it," she lamented. "I wore it to a Trudeau fundraiser a few years ago and felt absolutely magnificent."

I was confused. "Sage is having a gala?"

She honoured me with a tinkling laugh. "Alas, no. It's in Toronto. I fly out Friday morning."

I considered this. "Is that where you're from?" I perched on this dinky chaise lounge and felt tremendously Victorian.

"No. Vancouver. But I think I might move to TO; I have acquaintances there. Or maybe New York. I have acquaintances there, too."

I nodded like I knew what it was like to have a bevy of global acquaintances. "Why'd you move here, to dumb-ass old Sage, any-way?"

She was now draped in turquoise chiffon and swishing this way and that in front of the mirror, so I only saw her frown as a reflection. Was it for the way the gown hung, or my question? Either way, she quickly replaced the look with her usual poised mask.

"Oh, you know," she said nonchalantly, "there was a little trouble. You know," she repeated, wrinkling her pert nose and winking in a way that made it impossible for me to tell her that no, I don't know. An illegitimate pregnancy, perhaps? No, she was way past child-bearing age. More likely, it was the nasty divorce she'd hinted at.

Before we were done, Julia had slipped in and out of six more robes and even poured me into three that had freakin' hung on her. She was skinny to the point of gaunt and wore a padded brassiere to boot. I have boobs, but the dresses looked like cheap costumes on me.

Except the last one. It was black with tasteful gold swirly appliques that ran up the sides.

"Lovely," commented Julia after plucking at me for several moments. "You've a lovely bosom." So different than Germ's occasional *nice tits, Wiz*. "Take it, please. A girl should always have one black formal on hand, even diner waitresses from, where is it? Oh, yes, Dumb-ass Sage."

"Oh, I couldn't. Really." The garment surely cost more than my entire wardrobe and jewelry combined.

"No arguments. That dress has bad memories for me; if you don't take it, I'll just throw it out."

"Gee, thanks, Julia. Thank you. I'll take really good care of it, even if I never get to actually wear it anywhere."

"You could be a daredevil and get married in it," she suggested mischievously. "That would knock that young man of yours for a loop."

I must've made a face at the mention of Germ.

"What? Not Mr. Right? Good that you know it. Don't compromise; things will only get messy later on." Again with the messes. Interesting. "What do you want, Louise, truly want, from your young life?"

I squirmed and felt like a teenager playing dress-up. "I'm not sure. I . . . no, I'm not sure."

Her gaze was penetrating. "You do know. I can tell. Tell me when you're ready; maybe I can help." At that moment her bedside telephone rang, and I was able to wiggle back into my second-hand Levis, unscrutinized.

On my next day off, I went to the library and sat flipping through college calendars for two hours. It was overwhelming, the number of things a girl could study. As with the charity dress I'd stored in the back of the closet, I didn't report my research to Germ. Silence was relatively easy because I wasn't speaking to him during this period due to his purchase of a new welding torch that we could ill afford.

"Jesus, Germ! I was saving that money."

"For what? It's not like we're gonna have to buy a new heater this year." No, indeed; that was last year's savings.

I shook my head in frustration. "It doesn't matter for what. It's important to have some kind of nest egg, that's all."

"You get those smarts from the old lady next door?" he sneered in an uncharacteristic flash of snottiness.

"No!" I retorted, suddenly mad. "And she's not old. She's gorgeous. Mature gorgeous, not garage pin-up bimbo gorgeous, like you're used to."

Typically, he was grinning again already. That was his, our, specialty: he'd rile me up, then couldn't understand why I'd brood for hours while he'd instantly bounced back.

"Yeah, yeah. I met her the other day, jump-started that sporty little Datsun of hers. She looked pretty old to me. Nice rock on her finger, though."

"You didn't tell me you met her," I accused, angry that he'd made my duo a trio.

"No big deal; keep your gaunch on. I just gave her a boost when I saw her all distressed-like." He farted, and I winced. "I'm going over to Spider's for a while, check out his scrap metal."

"Don't you dare buy anything!" I yelled, picturing the stacked-up contents of the shed and backroom after similar trips to Spider's as he clumped across the porch. "And don't stay all damn day drinking moonshine, either. Don't think I don't know that still is up and running again, 'cause I do!" Deflated, I decided I needed a visit to Julia's.

Her chimes echoed twice before she came to the door, looking alarmingly plain.

"Julia, I'm sorry. It was rude of me to just drop by, but you see, Germ, well, he just makes me so mad . . ." I stopped my blathering. "Hey, are you okay? Are you sick?"

She waved an unadorned, unmanicured but still graceful hand. "No, darling. I just didn't sleep well last night. Would you like to step in?"

"Only if you're sure," I hedged, dying to get inside her serene walls again.

"It's Tony, you see," she explained when we were settled on her red leather couch, all the way from Italy, balancing cookies called biscotti and special frothy coffees she called lattes, on our laps. Her maid concocted them with special machines, also shipped from Italy. "I had to tell him goodbye, and he didn't take it very well. He was taking us far too seriously."

"Oh," I said, hoping it conveyed whatever she needed.

"Anyway, it's water under the bridge. You were saying that your young man has irritated you?"

My trouble seemed so boring compared to breaking off a fling with a hot young Italian. "Oh, he just went and spent my, well, our savings on a totally unnecessary thing."

"Oh, dear. And men call us frivolous spenders. My second husband collected antique guns at an exorbitant rate and price, yet argued over a measly few thousand dollars in the settlement. What were you saving for, Louise?"

I took a big mouthful of the strong coffee. Was it time to say my plans out loud? "School. I want to go to law school. Now, I have to start saving all over again."

"Forgive me, dear, but how much had you saved?"

Suddenly, I was acutely aware of the freakin' piggy bank I'd deemed my fortune. "Oh, not much. $267.00."

Julia pursed her lips. "Well, don't let this setback ruin your plans; an educated girl is an independent girl. I," she smiled wryly, laying a hand on her *cartilaginous* chest, "am finally independent, but it took three messy divorces."

Three!

"Julia, why did you move to Sage—I mean, I know you're thinking of going to Toronto or New York, but why Sage, so out of the blue?"

She tapped the rim of her cup with her stark nail and took a delicate sip before answering. "Foolishly, I upset some Vancouver acquaintances rather badly, along with my third ex-husband, in whose home I was still living. I was no longer welcome in the same social circles, so when I heard through the grapevine that this house was available, I said to myself, 'Julia, it's a sign to try suburbia for a while.' So I did. I offered to pay for the renovations—the owner thinks I have exquisite decorating taste—so he was more than happy to supply me with a hideaway for as long as need be."

"Well, I hope it need be for a long time," I offered, "because I'm really enjoying our friendship."

Julia looked taken aback, like I'd said something far too intimate. Finally, she rewarded me with a dazzling smile that stood out from her unpowdered face and uncombed hair.

"So, Germ," I said later that week, when I was talking to him again and he'd apologized repeatedly for splurging on the new tool by welding me a new magazine rack and door-knocker, and by fixing the back-porch swing—all things I'd been begging for. "I was wondering what you think, what you would think, if I took some courses at the college in January. Now, I don't even know if I can get in, but, um, well, I'd like to." I tried not to register that he was gouging out lint from his soup-bowl-sized navel.

"Sure, baby! Whatever you want. You mean, like, some secretary stuff or something? Will you have time, with the jobs and all?"

This was the bit where extreme patience would be needed. I'd practised with Julia and in front of the mirror. "Well now, Germ, that's the thing. You'd need to get a job."

"Well, baby, I'd love to do that for you, but my trades licence is expired now, so I wouldn't be able to get on anywhere worthwhile. And you know I'm waiting to hear back about that contract to design that sculpture at City Hall. I want to be available to take it on."

I was ready for this point. "Germ, that tender was put out four months ago. Either they're not going to do the project, or it was awarded to someone else. Someone actually qualified." Ooops, that wasn't part of my script.

"Actually qualified?" he repeated, aghast.

"Not that you're not good. I just meant, someone with a current welding licence, maybe some kind of art degree. Like that. Not that you're not good." He looked only marginally convinced. "Besides, what I meant by job, was just that—job. Any job. Like the three, any-job kinds of jobs I've had for the majority of our time together."

Keep to the issue, Julia had coached.

"That old woman has completely changed you," he accused.

I considered refuting this. "Maybe. But so what? I'm going to be something. After all, an educated girl is an independent girl."

His troubled face was oddly adorable. I moved in close. "Germ, I'm starting a journey. Come with me."

We spent a quiet evening watching *The Waltons* on the least-fuzzy channel before making distracted love and falling asleep.

No one was more surprised than me when Julia, pristine and coiffed, stepped into the diner near the end of my Thursday shift.

"Julia! Great to see you, but you know we don't serve brie here, and the closest thing to pâté I could muster up is hamburger in a blender," I teased. She made a playful face at me.

"I was interested to learn how the discussion went, but if now is not a good time . . ." Suddenly, she seemed to become aware of her cheesy, greasy surroundings.

"Gosh, no, it's a great time. I missed my break, so let me check if I can get off early."

I stuck my head into the kitchen and yelled for Bill, the manager. "Listen, Bill, my friend's here; can I skip out early instead of claiming the missed break?"

I received an affirmative grunt and skipped back to Julia, who'd been drawn into the ramblings of one of the regulars, a wino truck driver who sobered up in our backroom.

"Ralph, leave my friend alone. She's out of your league." Gently, I guided Julia to the least-graffitied booth.

"You said 'friend,' three times," she said, perplexed.

"Well, yeah, I mean, it just came out like . . . huh?"

"You say it so naturally."

"I meant it. Does it offend you?" Maybe she didn't want me bellowing out our relationship in public.

"Heaven's, Louise, no. I'm flattered. I haven't been honoured with the title too often in my life, especially as an adult. Unfortunately, circumstances have frequently been. . . ."

"Messy?" I finished, and she smiled. I'd have to develop a tougher line of questioning if I wanted to make it as a lawyer. "Anyway, I'm sorry I didn't pop over with the news, after your help and all, but I picked up extra shifts of everything. I want to make enough to start school, *college,* in January."

Saying it gave me the good goosebumps.

"The discussion went okay. I mean, we didn't fight over it— not too badly, anyway. He hasn't told me if he's getting a job or not, and I don't know what I'm going to do if he doesn't. But, I phoned for the application papers anyway, and they might even get here tomorrow."

"That's really wonderful; truly exciting." She paused and tapped the scarred Formica table. "I have a confession. Your young man came over yesterday."

"He did? He didn't tell me. What'd he want?"

She patted my hand. "I think he just wanted to check out the old bird. Goodness, don't worry; I'm just supposing those were the words in his head. Anyway, he wanted to talk to the person with whom his 'Wizzie' was such good friends. His pretence was to ask me if I needed anything welded."

I relaxed, rolled my eyes, and we both giggled.

"He's very handsome," she continued. "When he boosted my battery, he looked a little scruffier."

I winced. "Yesterday? Yeah, he kinda cleaned up 'cause he'd been down to City Hall to ask them about . . . oh, never mind. He's no John Travolta, but he's okay."

"John Travolta? Do I know him?"

"The actor. He's in a new movie called *Saturday Night Fever.* Total hunk."

"Ah. I shall watch out for him. But now, I must run, Louise. I'm going Christmas shopping. When you have three ex-husbands, the family list gets quite lengthy. One divorces the man, not his family."

I thought I knew why she was really leaving. In a weird way, I hoped that someday I, too, would feel uncomfortable sitting in a slashed-up, orange vinyl booth.

The college application came in the next morning's mail. After poring over the brochures and schedules and forms for a good hour, I thought I needed Julia's calm and logical input. It was snowing lightly, but I shoved my feet into old sneakers and crashed through the shrubbery that separated our houses. Germ had said he was going out job-hunting. I could only pray he was just killing time at Spider's, best-case scenario.

The *pooh-pooh* chimes didn't respond when I pushed the button. Even though I loudly knocked three times, neither Julia nor the maid came to the door. I peered through the garage window, saw her shiny Datsun, and started worrying. I knew she wasn't really that old, forty-five or so, but I couldn't help thinking she'd had some kind of accident. Falling down stairs or slipping in the bathtub could happen to anyone.

I knocked on the door two more times, dancing around a little to keep the cold at bay, before I tried the knob. As I suspected, Julia thought suburban living meant crime-free: the door was unlocked. I stood in the foyer silently, uncomfortable entering Julia's house uninvited. It was chic and bare when she was a welcoming presence beside me; without her, the house was downright austere. I was just about to call out when I heard her.

"Jeremy! Jeremy, bring the wine when you come back to bed, darling. There's an open bottle of Chablis in the refrigerator."

It took me a moment, the name being as foreign-sounding as "Louise" had been before I met Julia. I stood still, but for my trembling knees.

"I don't see any wine," bellowed the familiar voice. "Where d'you say it was?"

"On the second shelf. I think it's lying down, beside the pâté."

"Yeah, yeah," Germ called back. "Got it."

I heard him clomp back upstairs. I didn't need any more information, and I most certainly didn't want to see anything more. Yet I found myself in the hallway outside Julia's *ajar* bedroom door. Hell! Her plain old half-open door. Suddenly, I didn't want to have anything to do with her world, not even her vocabulary.

"I don't think I'd like pâté," Germ was whingeing. "Isn't it pig guts or something?"

"Yes, you would and no, it's not," assured Julia. "It's a rich man's food, for which, as I understand, you should start acquiring a taste. It sounds like Louise is on her way to financial security."

"Who . . ." he started, before realizing. "Oh, yeah. Her."

Her? I charged in.

"You mother f'ing—practically literally—prick!" Thank God Julia was wearing some kind of peignoir and that Germ, totally naked, was only fiddling with the wine cork.

"Oh, my God," said Julia with infuriating dignity.

"Shit! Wizzie. What're you doing here?" yelped Germ, scrambling to cover bits of himself I'd seen a million times.

Not able to focus on either of them, I chose some fancy-smancy painting that hung above Julia's headboard.

"What am I doing here? Oh, I don't know. I come sometimes

to visit my friend, Julia. I won't ask the same of you, because it's friggin' clear what you're doing here, so . . ."

My voice was cracking and squeaking like the screen door.

"Gee, Wiz . . ."

"Louise, I'm so sorry. It just happened. It's all my fault; don't blame Jeremy."

"Y'know, Julia, I realize the concept of 'friend,' for whatever reason, is pig Latin to you, but it's a pretty basic concept that a forty-five-year-old *friend* doesn't sleep with her *friend's* twenty-four-year-old partner."

"I'm fifty-three," contributed Julia in a rare moment of candidness.

Germ gasped.

"Please, Louise, hate me, but if you love this man, forgive him. I swear to you, it was all me; I seduced him. I invited him in the other day when he came asking about you; I begged him to come back today."

Germ said nothing, damned if he agreed or not.

Now I understood all of Julia's past "messes."

Tony, the ill-fated black dress in the back of my closet, losing grace within her Vancouver social circle, the divorces.

"Julia, take your hoity-toity self out of my life. And Germ, as your landlady, get the hell out of my house while I'm at work tonight."

To be sure, it wasn't a good day for Juicy Burger customers.

Within three days, Julia's driveway was the drive-in movie of activity it'd been four months before. I stood shivering at the mailbox, watching men cart out the red leather couch, the plants from the solarium that would never survive a freakin' freezing journey in the back of a moving truck. Within the dozen cardboard boxes

I saw just in those few minutes were the special machines from Italy, the gowns, the crystal wine goblets, and the Royal Doulton serving plates, all of which I'd touched. She was off, I assumed, to Toronto or New York, to all those damn acquaintances.

It all happened so fast, it was bizarre.

Later that night, Julia's house was dark, her tasteful renovations all for naught, the house as much a decorated shell as Julia herself. When I let myself into the cabin after my museum shift, I saw that a fat envelope had been shoved under the ill-sealed door. It was, of course, addressed to me in Julia's fine, lacy handwriting.

My dear friend, Louise,

I ask for no forgiveness or understanding, as I have neither for myself. I never wanted to hurt you. I don't know why I do what I do, only that I cannot say I will never do it again. Please accept this gift, the only kind I can give. Go forward to true independence. Julia.

In a second envelope was a substantial cheque made out to Sage College, and five thousand smackeroos.

Outside, a gust of wind caught the screen door and wrenched it off its hinges. Again.

Objections in
the Dark

Martini and Underhill were starting their routine. The crowd, Saddam *et al* about to be temporarily spun out of their minds, went crazy at the first strands of that song about time, by the Righteous Brothers. Cassandra could never remember the actual name; it was from Demi Moore's movie where she played the potter with the dead husband. Anyway, it didn't matter, because just then the power went out. No, back on. No, out. Yes. Out for sure.

The defense rests, Your Honour.

Cass had been so busy flipping back and forth between the skating and an ancient Ingrid Bergman movie, all while avoiding CNN, that she hadn't even noticed the storm come up, let alone how lethal it had become.

Cassandra was frequently caught off-guard like this, a humiliating proviso for a lawyer.

She sat in blackness as thick as oil. The gales of wind outside shrieked: the sound of ravaged women.

Her skin prickled. A shot of cold air came blasting in from somewhere, like someone had opened a door to the frigid outside, but she was alone. Cass wondered whether the electricity being off meant the electric heat would be off too. Hmmm. *Duh*. Pretty stupid. If John were here, he would roll his eyes and let go one of his "typical untechnical woman" comments. Well, she just wouldn't have brought it up if he was here, which he wasn't. Never had been, in fact. Cass was very good at monitoring her outbursts and queries in his presence, far better than when in court. But when she was alone, the thoughts really zinged around her head, then out her mouth like little missiles of stupidity, insecurity, or silliness.

She smelled grease, an acrid, permeating stench that made her nose twitch. If she could twitch like Sabrina, she'd put the power back on.

Among other pesky things that needed to be *on* or *off*, instead of at a lukewarm simmer.

Anyway! First things first. Cass stood up tentatively and looked in the general direction of the TV.

Yippee—no home aerobics video tonight.

Candles. She needed candles. Easy. Ever-ready flickers of romance or sedation were part of her wishfully alluring décor.

Matches were another story.

She knew there wasn't a single flint in her suite; she remembered a wild scramble for a light quite some time ago, the last time

she'd tried to cook a proper, grown-up, sit-down supper for someone. Someone? She knew damn well who.

The witness is directed to answer the question.

No, wait, that'd been back in the city. Any subsequently discovered dog-eared matchbooks, socks with holes, paper plates, bars
of hotel soap, and hoarded yogurt containers hadn't made the
packing cut.

And yet, she'd slipped other useless baggage back in at the last
minute while burly movers stood by impatiently, possibly picking
their teeth with her discarded matchbook covers. Things such as
too-small lingerie, plastic Coquilles St. Jacques dishes, wool from
an abandoned afghan project.

A hundred-and-seventy-two-pound investment broker named
John.

Cass made a mental note to throw her loose change into a gas
station receptacle that would entitle her to a handful of matchbooks, which she vowed to strew strategically throughout the
basement dwelling. Matches seemed safer than a lighter: if she
broke down and bought a lighter (a buck twenty-nine at the
Irving Station), she'd take up smoking. Again. In a heartbeat.

Like she took back up with brokers.

Cassandra climbed the stairs to the main foyer. The people
upstairs, her landlords, were gone.

Grady and Betsy: hokey-pokey names that matched everything about the rent-collectors. It irked Cass that they called her
their boarder. She didn't eat with them, didn't want to, given the
various incarnations of grease G&B consumed. She only used their
laundry soap, for God's sake, and otherwise kept to herself.

Full disclosure!

She balanced the stench of fish sticks with burned popcorn fumes. If only there hadn't been such a housing shortage in this worn-out little town in the first place. . . .

Cass groped her way across the kitchen, wondering where such a couple would keep matches. They didn't smoke either: they ate jujubes, which was just as well because Cass got very judgmental towards people who were fat *and* smoked. One vice per person, please.

Grady, a redhead with a birthmark shaped like Saudi Arabia on his left cheek, was a handy-dandy type of guy. He'd have a stash of flashlights somewhere, chock full of new batteries. She giggled inexplicably; Grady probably had a big, miner-type hard hat. Its beam would make Cassandra's tiny space below as bright and penetrated as a night movie shoot.

She drew the line at venturing out to the shed. It had creeped her out ever since they found a nutso in combat clothes hiding out in there. Imagine making it all the way from the Shearwater Base without being reported? Apparently, the peon was pissed that he didn't get picked for Kuwait.

And, the shed smelled like dog poo.

She shuffled across their kitchen, a few terse words for G&B's spoiled mutt on the way. Wasn't it enough for her to trip over the bulky creature in broad daylight, as it straddled the back porch steps?

Cass thought about having to reset all the clocks because of the power outage. There was nothing more annoying than watching the spastic clock on the VCR flash on and off, *12:00, 12:00, 12:00,* calling her from concentrating on anything else, even if she was in another room. She swore to get all the clocks in sync this time, instead of rushing around in the mornings, late according to the alarm, on time by the microwave, and forty minutes early according to the stove. And *12:00, 12:00, 12:00* by the VCR.

Timing was everything.

She bumbled back downstairs, gripping the banister as if she were suffering a grave injury, and found her way into the basement proper, only a slightly more bearable destination than the shed. She started feeling around Grady's shelves, none too organized.

Objection!

Withdrawn, Your Honour: not organized at all.

She'd only been in there once before, when she needed a hammer for hanging pictures. Well, *more* of a hammer. Hers had come in a kit when she was ten years old and had been dabbling in some Barbie doll house-building extravaganza. All the other kiddie tools were missing now, or perhaps in her mother's crawl-space in the box marked Cassie's Baby Toys. Still, the puny hammer cracked Christmas peanuts adequately.

Pat. pat. pat.

She felt around the workbench with dainty pats, hoping not to impale her palm on a spike. That'd be dandy. Freezing, relocated, dislocated, jilted, *and* bloody. . . .

Had there been blood on the woman, the bedraggled one hunched over in the corner of the parking lot? The one who'd disappeared in the nanosecond between Cass's glance up and down, while digging for her keys? She'd been prepared to go over, to offer assistance, but where had the woman gone?

A brainstorm! The *key*-keys, the full set with her personal ones, the one to the office, and the other to John's apartment which she'd secretly copied, were presently MIA, but it took checking only three jacket pockets to find the spares. Wearing a pair of Grady's boots, Cass headed outside, making sure she did not lock herself out.

She could only wish for grander daily foresight.

Lightning jagged across the sky, taunting her with fleeting light. One thousand one, one thousand two. The thunder cracked open Cassie's skull, shuddered down her spine, ricocheted off the frozen ground and settled with a thud in the pit of her gut.

Mr. Hussein, is it still your testimony that man holds the ultimate power?

In her car, she pawed around for her mag-light, placed in the glove compartment last spring in a rare moment of organizational fortitude. It had only been used once, to assist some frantic and inept wedding DJ in a furious search through his battered shoeboxes of cassettes for "Sea of Love" before bewildered couples drifted off the dance floor.

But the glove compartment would not open. As she thumped away at the lock, Cass remembered cramming in three gas coupons, a brochure on skydiving, and a Cracker Jack box, say, three weeks ago. They'd combined forces, sprung up, and blocked the lock. She grimaced in remembrance of a similar routine the previous week—a mad search for a hairbrush—and how she had vowed at *that* time to clear out the car.

Her whole life needed purging.

As she probed around, Cass concluded that she could survive in the Sentra for an indeterminate length of time. It held a blanket (from the beach in the summer, still sandy), various half-bottles of (flat) Diet Coke, and one almost-full spring water from the day she'd felt especially healthful.

Is my learned colleague suggesting health is equal to virtue?

There was a box of crackers under the seat, along with scattered cassettes ranging from Melissa Etheridge to Yanni, the newest *Cosmo*, and—*hey!*—wedged in the crux of the back seat, a packaged condom.

One could live on less.

Cass scrambled back inside, the ferocious January wind beating at her and forcing her to grip the car door, the screen door, and the house door, for fear of them flying off their hinges into the next county. She discovered her *key*-keys in the door lock, abandoned because of the afternoon's armload of groceries and inebrients.

Good thing the Crown Prosecutor Selection Committee (Extraordinaire) hadn't witnessed that blunder.

Downstairs in the creepy basement again, Cass *pat, pat, pat* along the window ledge.

Success at last! She fingered the crusty casing and discovered it contained three whole matches. They sufficed to light two living room candles, and she gloated ridiculously in her success.

For the record, state your full name and Girl Guide affiliation.

Cass plunked cross-legged on the couch and wondered if it were worthwhile to get up and inspect the thermostat. No. She focused on the wavering candles before her, considering blowing one out in case the storm raged on indefinitely. Maybe.

Ridiculous woman, channelled John.

She'd mouthed the same sentiment at the immigrant—sorry, *new* Canadian—perched on the railing that corralled the frozen pizzas in Safeway. *Ridiculous woman. Get off the display.*

Whoosh! went the heavens.

Click! went her memory.

Jesus-smeesus, that was the woman with the bloody shoulder in the 7-Eleven parking lot.

The town wasn't that small, so why would Cass see her twice like that?

She shook her head to settle the SSG pellets that reverberated within her skull.

The temperature was definitely dropping; a flame held to the thermostat confirmed it was down to an old-fashioned sixty-eight degrees Fahrenheit. She tried to calculate to Celsius. Minus 30 . . . plus five, wasn't it? Damn. What was the formula? She could give up and go to bed under layers of sweatpants, quilts, and bath towels until Mr. Mulroney declared a state of emergency. Perhaps not Mulroney. Probably just the Mayor of Port Boot, or the lugubrious reigning Mountie.

Cass eyed the wood stove longingly. She sighed heavily, cognizant that it only added aesthetic value to the room (a rustic theme that wasn't even her style). Besides, what would she burn, the equally rustic wood panelling, so dark and lacquered that the suite was perpetually gloomy?

On a whim, Cass picked up the phone receiver, was serenaded with crackling and buzzing, and quickly hung up. She would have phoned Susan, to come for wine, to talk.

To confess to. Okay, so the reason I keep jamming on Country Bumpkin Bingo Night is that this dickhead, who I prefer to call the love of my life, keeps calling from the city and inviting me up to bang at the last minute.

And I go.

Kaboom! The sky regurgitated more evil.

Maybe it was better to jump in the car and drive to the only urban–like structure for a million miles, the 7-Eleven. She could read *Popular Mechanics* or *Seventeen* or *Rural Fuckin' Crafts*, eating the grotesque local hit, dill pickle potato chips. Or work, she could go to work. Surely the courthouse was on some kind of generator system. Then again, she already endlessly complained about the hateful hours spent there.

It was torturously unfair that John was only three hours away, at a murder mystery party, playing the doctor in a city that probably still had power. She knew the doctor bit, because that was why he was running out the door when she'd called, at 5:37, actually *looking* for an invite up this time. Or a halfway rendezvous. Cass wondered if the hosts had supplied a character as a date—was there a quirky nurse role within the box of mystery? Perhaps, Cass vamped, she should just show up, a mysterious, uninvited vixen.

And after, when characters and motives were clear, those they mutually knew would nod and ahem and murmur, "She's *not* still chasing our precious John?"

At the very least, it was unfair that he was warm, surrounded by people, and no doubt well into the CC and water. Cass wondered if she would even cross his mind tonight, indeed, if ever again. She palmed the window, icy and shuddering.

There were always the gifts by which he'd have to remember her: the Lamborghini poster, the cutesy laundry bag. Surely he couldn't look at those things without a pang, should her case for them be dismissed.

The court thanks the jury for its time and dedication.

Then there was the matter of the next weekend. The Crown Prosecutor's thing. Cass had agreed months ago to accompany Davis, a perfectly nice, suitable, emotionally available, super-skinny colleague. She'd felt triumphant saying yes to Davis, giddy over annihilating John from her life with a hard kiss to Davis's chicken lips.

But John had called and his voice—it probably had something to with the Monty Python impression—buckled her fortitude and she returned them to their bimonthly fling. If she could just stay strong, stop being such a suction cup, clinging to what would never be. Stop being a five-foot-one, 109-pound garden slug that laboured in and out of his life, docile as hell and deliberately always leaving behind sticky gunk as evidence of her existence.

Cassie felt a warm pulse on her chin. She'd been unconsciously picking at a pimple she swore had been there since tenth grade. How attractive. Indeed, that was one benefit of sleeping alone, of knowing no one would drop into her hick-town bed, ever-guarded by the doughy gossipmongers upstairs: one could go to bed quite comfortably bound in curlers or socks and mittens lined with Vaseline or quadruple layers of zit-zapper.

Depressing, to have the opportunity to become beautiful, night, after night, after night.

Outside, while the skies continued to crackle and clap with vicious glee, Cass thought of the war coverage on the evening news. Night, after night, after night.

Nothing to do with her.

Unconscionably, even wars spurned jokes. Oil jokes. Missile jokes. Shouldn't they be taboo? She'd heard a few (dozen) supposed yuks. Like AIDS or space shuttle jokes, somebody always carved out some crass quip within twenty-four hours.

Cassandra was chilled but sleepy, in the state where the decision to rouse or be falsely lulled, aided by the last dribbles of wine, was impossible to make. It was like having to pee in the middle of the night and debating whether to get up or not. What was worth it? Which represented less pain?

Suddenly, the wine ran cold through her veins.

That woman.

The suspect is identified for the record.

Was it possible the parking lot woman and the frozen-food woman were the woman in the Halifax nightclub? Was she being followed? The more she considered it, the more Cass was convinced it was the same dark, ruminating young woman, watching her chug Keith's draft with people from the old office. Yes. It seemed obvious now. Who was she? The abandoned wife of some idiot she'd put away? That would figure. Thank God that woman's unnerving stare had faded with each beer, had disappeared completely once Cass slipped into the oh-what-the-hell world of intoxication and shouted to the woman, *What do you want from me?* This outburst, she recalled, greatly amused her equally drunken friends.

She pulled together all the evidence.

The same waif was on the slate-coloured winter beach where Cass had stood lamenting why John couldn't, wouldn't, shouldn't commit. Why, she'd blubbered, after all the lingerie and home-made sweet-and-sour chicken and cooing (albeit, with forced rapture) at his past and present hurts, why wasn't it within her power to make him love her?

On the beach that day, the strange woman had said something like, "They came for my man yesterday, to fight, though he only sells carpets. I think now he will be dead soon." Cass had given her head a fierce shake and driven carefully home from the beach, repeatedly instructing herself that she'd read the line in *Maclean's*.

She reached out to adjust the listing candle in the quaking basement suite and gasped.

Goddammit!

Order, order in the court!

The woman! In her house! Just out of reach at the end of the couch. Jesus! Two ragamuffins clung to the stalker's dark caftan.

"How did you get in my house? Get out of my house!"

"My name is Azima. My storm is not created by our God, but by governments."

Cassandra shrank into the couch, terrified.

I am cracking up. My God, I'm totally cracking up.

Cass's relatives lived halfway across the country. Her grand-mother had phoned that morning with a steady prattle of family gossip: her sister had moved to a penthouse apartment with floor-to-ceiling windows (gunfire would blast them out easily enough); Cousin Liz miscarried; Cassandra's mother would be home from Pennsylvania shortly.

Does Counsel have a point, Your Honour?

Cass had touched briefly on her new work responsibilities, the only topic she could easily lie about. "I'll write more in a letter. I said *I'll write*. I'll write a LET-TER."

Crap connection. She'd hung up feeling sorry for herself: there was no one on the east coast who'd known her for more than three years, but in truth, it was more comfortable to keep people distant. Cass justified that they couldn't magically change her life, so why worry them that Port Boot was her last chance? Let them go on about the charred condition of her toaster oven or the explosive state of the linen closet during yearly visits—better than probing too closely into what was actually her life. Actually. Her. Life.

I'll make my point shortly, Your Honour.

Now she'd have to hide weird visits from phantom Arab women as well.

Cass squeezed her eyes open and shut, repeatedly, rapidly, to dissolve the image of the woman who seemed lit from within. As if she had swallowed a candle.

Of course, no police could be called. How could she explain? She'd lose all credibility defending their cases.

She forced her mind back to John, a welcome distraction for once.

They were supposed to meet next week after the CP soiree. For a friendly fuck, so to speak. Cass considered not calling him as planned, perhaps exhausting herself with the emaciated Davis. It would be a grand experiment to see if John even noticed, to see if he would call upon her return to Port Boot Probational Purgatory and ask what happened.

Oh-ho-ho, but there was risk in that. He might not register being ditched at all; he might interpret it as simple oversight, a mere busyness on her part and not the principled gesture the silence actually meant.

Counsellor's rambling again.

Anyway, that decision was a week away. She needn't even think about it until Friday night, say, ten o'clock, while holed up in her government-approved, appropriately discounted hotel room. She might be locked up by then anyway.

If she could just keep focused on his vagueness toward her coy request for personalized bed and breakfast services for the weekend, once a standard joke. Obviously, not any more.

Ambivalence: her drug of choice. Cass knew she made Dr. Dolittle's Push-Me Pull-You animal look decisive.

Her mind snapped back to reality. The refrigerator. Having long ago defied—or defiled—a culinary heritage, she knew its complete contents in an instant. Ketchup. Oranges hard enough to be lobbed from cannons. An egg-white face mask. In another hour, she'd open the fridge door and heat the living room.

She thought about doing some sit-ups (to keep warm, not fit), but that dragged her back to torturous deliberations about exchanging a perfectly sculptured body for a commitment. It was irrelevant, she hoped, and would no doubt be an exercise in humiliation and failure anyway. No wonder she had difficulty convincing judges of an accused's guilt; she couldn't even convince herself of anything.

Cass held the candle up to the thermostat. Sixty-four degrees. Time for Action. (Wasn't that her motto, when she'd accepted the "transfer" a month ago?)

The phone was within her reach. She briefly considered rechecking for a dial tone, dialling John's number, if only to hear his voice on the answering machine. Maybe she'd leave a bright, chirpy message, maybe just a maddening click.

"You have choices," Azima reminded gently from her shadowy position in the corner of the room. "As many choices as there are grains of rice in a spoonful."

Cassandra yelped and dropped the candle. Hot wax penetrated her jeans.

At that moment, the house convulsed under an outside attack—a real explosion, powerful enough to shatter her ground-level windows and punch a wave of heat into the living room. Then there was just light, which cast an eerie, flickering reflection on the television screen. What the hell?

A bomb? A firecracker from the gods to get her off her ass?

Cass glanced around for Azima. Gone. Smart woman.

She blew out the candles, bundled up, and ascended the stairs to investigate.

Cass peered around the back corner of the house. In the front yard, people camouflaged in toques and upturned collars—some brave ones wore only bathrobes—were already gathering around a mangled, blistering weapon. A Pinto had actually pierced Grady and Betsy's living room; its driver was splayed across the trunk. Most of him. As fast as his blood gushed out, the wind whisked it into the air and repositioned it as demented spray paintings in the snow.

Grady and Betsy pulled into the driveway.

Strangely, Cass felt claustrophobic. She wore Grady's boots again, and her own down jacket. She fumbled in the pockets for mittens and found none. It didn't matter; her insides were explosively hot. She pulled her arms out of the sleeves and buried her hands in her steaming armpits. Unseen, she stumbled across the backyard, through the abutting neighbour's property, and onto the next street. She trotted until the fire in her gut was smothered by inhaling icy air. Then she doubled over, choked out hot mucus.

Streetlights, porch-lights, and TVs sprang into life around her, as if her passing presence sliding down the road made a difference. As if.

"You have choices." Someone's blasting television?

No, Azima in her simple covering, oblivious to the storm.

Cass trudged back to help at the accident scene.

Three hours later, the telephone lines restored, Cass said a clear goodbye to a groggy John. She tried not to dwell on how relieved he'd sounded once he woke up; she concentrated on how strong she felt.

From her toasty bed at an ungodly hour, Cass willed Azima to appear, to tell the messenger that she'd listened after all. She'd heard.

That she'd chosen.

But she saw nothing but blackness, heard only fading wind.

Drinking Dreams on Granville

Drinks wine of tawny-coloured silk —no, wait!—*smoky*, tawny-coloured silk, like the swatch has been penetrated by a single, spiralling, campfire exhale. Feels spirally herself; naturally would after chugging wine on a stomach earlier scraped raw by black coffee. Spirally and swishy. Favourite feeling.

Sits alone at an outside patio, within a row of metal tables and chairs chained together like tour group luggage outside a Four Seasons. Girl at table behind assures friend she could just *live* in sandals 365 days a year. Man of the couple ahead returns lady friend's roast beef dip for being too pink.

For oozing too much cow.

Didi's not eating. If she wanted something, she'd have opened a can of tuna and pressed it into mouldy pita bread at home. Wants wine. Food binds; wine frees.

Wants escape.

Plans to the play The Game, as soon as the wine's massaged her head just a little more, to the perfect malleability. Called "The What If?" Game.

Her lover's flying right now, in a buddy's ultralight. For all she knows, they're right above her and Skyler's looking down through science-fiction-strength binoculars, going, "Christ, that's my woman, getting shit-faced at noon in a seedy Granville Street bar." How mad could he get, way up there?

No matter. Way, way, *way* more important is how mad he'd get on earth.

Not a really seedy bar. Granted, bar's on Granville Street, between Nelson and Smythe—the part the city's supposed to be cleaning up—so yeah, yeah, a bit dodgey, the kinda hole that changes names and management like Skyler changes moods, but not much else wrong with it. Really. Likes it here. Close to home, wine $3.25 a glass.

What If . . . the police and ambulances're on the tarmac now? In Abbottsford. A guess: don't know exactly where they went. Officials running around, picking up limbs and black-box bits. ID free-flying in the breeze. Wonders if he got his address changed on his driver's licence, or if the cops'll go to the old apartment on Bute. Didi didn't switch over either; hers is actually expired. Can't stand to have pictures taken no more. Been over a year since buying the condo in the new waterfront building.

Since Skyler bought the condo. Big present, that.

Fast-forward. Five o'clock in the afternoon. Home. What If . . . intercom buzzer rings.

"Yes," says Didi impatiently, irked that Skyler hasn't called, and in a further altered state. How's'ee gonna miss one joint? Fuck, there's a good twenty tight-rolled doobies in the tiki box. She *so* deserves just one.

"Vancouver Police," a deep voice says, and Didi'd know. They don't come in person to yak about broken legs or drunk driving charges. Or flying hot water.

No. Don't like this. Skyler ever found out she thought that about him? Do a shitload more than bust up the new forty-pack of Ikea dishes.

Skip ahead. Mississauga. Carries his urn of ashes real solemnly in a memorial ceremony, fawned over by the world. Plus, would've told that stupid shoe-store manager she ain't starting work on Monday after all. That'd be a good thing. Gonna get fired shortly anyway. Boss'd say it was work habits, but it'd be for the same reason as always. Ugly Useless Bitch. Ask Skyler. Ask the mirror.

Sips more smoky wine on Granville Street. Tries to sip. People zip by like ants on their way to a dead mouse. Can tell the tour bus people in an instant. The women wear their thick vinyl purse straps across them like beauty pageant ribbons (Yay, Miss Oklahoma; Yay, Miss Fucking Freak Face), and have recently permed hair; the men cradle packs like bulbous, gaseous stomachs after eating tainted coastal oysters. Two lapel pricks visible, little fang marks, where nametags get pinned. Sometimes they keep the plastic identities on.

Like Didi'd ever need a tag. Skyler reminded her who she was all the time.

Two foreign specimens going by now. Not really into Danielle Steele—always gotta have a shield—so she just listens.

"But the guide says 'be sure to always carry an umbrella', George. You read it too. It better be on the bus and not in the suite, and it better not rain."

Brilliant, stellar day, clear and sure. Sun beats into The Mark, makes it as slick and shiny as melting plastic.

"It's not going to rain, Lydia. We won't need the umbrella. You feeling like lunch yet?" They stop, Lydia to paw through her beige wicker purse and George to re-tie his white golf shoes.

"I shouldn't be hungry," she clucks. "After that, what was it called again, George?"

"West Coast Egg Explosion," reminds George, checking his watch. "We only got a half-hour."

"Let's just get a snack then," Lydia decides. "Surely to God this city has some low-fat potato chips and I'm really, truly dying for a diet cola."

"We didn't get down to see the Pan Pacific Hotel," bemoans George.

"There, there's a store," announces Lydia. "Surely to God they have low-fat potato chips. Cross now, George, there's no cars."

Bye-bye tour people.

Drinks and sighs. At least it's not snowing and there're no beavers roaming Granville, a US of A misconception that gnawed its way into the twenty-first century.

What If . . . her Lotto numbers get drawn in Winnipeg, or wherever those balls live? Pretty blonde chick calls out 0-0-0-0-0-0.

No. No fair to play that one. Bought no tickets.

What If . . . that man there—the one between Didi and them with the bleeding cow sandwich—leans over, asks to share a table?

"Excuse me, Miss, do you have a light?" he asks. "I lost my last flame to the breeze."

"No, no sorry," Didi explains, holds up empty hands, like she owes him concrete proof.

Nods understandingly. "You must be a west-coaster, so healthy."

Didi titters. She'd angle her face away? No. Straight on, look at him freaking straight on. "You're not from here?" Got a craggy face. Yes, craggy. Never use that word.

"No, I'm from New York. Here on business. You?"

"PR."

"No kidding! I'm the marketing director for Prego."

Proceeds to get bogged down in trite dialogue. F'ing goes this way sometimes, ends up slamming the game shut like a Scrabble board, like a pissed eight-year-old.

Screw it. Doesn't make eye contact with Mr. Man. Eye contact literally. Eye as in one *eye*. The other lists left too much. Gets up for another glass of wine, leaves $6.95 paperback upside down on the table, ripped denim shirt on the chair. Tables are premium: must be protected. Not like people.

Waits at the counter for her turn. What If . . . the bar tart says she's gotta order something to eat with her wine. There're a lot of liquor rules about who can serve what and when and how. Big, big-huge bullshit political argument about the size and numbers of TVs a joint could have; raged on for months. Already had one drink, she defends, why didn't someone tell her that then?

Stop.

Sounds drunk and argumentative; it'd make their point completely. They'd throw her out. Who'd want a drunk, scarred, soon-to-be-fired shoe-seller around?

Bar tart doesn't ask a thing, just pours wine to the imaginary line that's different in each bar, for every waitress. Adds it to Didi's bill.

Meanders back to the table, passes dozens of undeveloped

chicks smothered in hollandaise sauce. They watch her, each one. Eye to eye.

Mr. Man's gone now. Probably a perverted old fart anyhow or a plain old West End fruit. In another life, always made them casting agents, but OD'd on that one. Totally unrealistic now.

In this life, usually they were plastic surgeons 'cause all the makeup in the world don't cover The Mark. Tried a million times. Skyler said give it up. You're finished.

Gotta create daydreams with a chance. Otherwise, they turn into day-depressions. Got those happening, too.

Fuck sipping. Takes a gulp. Downs 'er by a third.

3-3-3.

6-6-6.

People're really flowing by now, some hollandaise, some smoky, some rare meat. Lotsa second and third generation immigrants. Heads, as black and shellacked as licorice gob-stoppers, speak slangy and saucy Canadian, sometimes ultra-timid *heh-ros* while clutching upside-down maps from ESL schools. Flawless skin. Can never tell 'til you embarrass the shit out of yourself, talking like a deaf retard to them. She freaks them out. Probably hide people like her in their countries.

What If . . . the street's in . . . Istanbul. No, too much skin-flashing going down to be Istanbul. Rio? Go to Rio and teach English in the mornings and lie on Copacabana Beach all afternoon. Be anonymous. Be one of the Ugly Beautiful People.

Something would happen in Rio. Something's not happening here. Skyler burns up all energy.

Breezy now. One of the mysterious red *Repent Sinner* signs flutters around, wraps around her chair leg, strangles itself. Didi frees it.

Lets the last drop evaporate, drop she can never get no matter how many times she tilts back, extends her tongue. Pays her bill with money from the grocery jar and leaves. Crosses Granville against the light 'cause really, who doesn't? Gets fingered by a bus driver and cursed at by a thirty-year-old on a scooter.

Cuts across the back lot, a shortcut to the apartment, doesn't look down. Maggoty seagull's probably still there; plus, three times she caught homeless men squatting, shitting. Lately some restaurant's been dumping gooey leftovers.

Plus plain old garbage.

Feeling peevish. Can't get into What If . . . today; only got real things to think about, like making something different than macaroni from macaroni. Laundry up the yin-yang. Goddamn shoe-store job. Why bother? Accusations'd start right quick; Skyler'd come in and make a scene. Plus, got no good clothes.

He might be home by now, might not. Either way, he'll arrive, all pumped-up. No matter how many times she speaks to the cop or how many planes she boards to Ontario, he'll arrive.

'Cause Skyler's a doer. Got all the energy. Thing with the boiling spaghetti water's a good example.

Unfortunate, that her face got in the way.

Wine swish's wearing off. Shit. Wants to feel swishy when he comes home and notices the empty money jar. Checks all the time.

Gotta buy a lottery ticket.

The Full Brazilian

Naked, but for a Red Deer College '91 T-shirt hitched up to my rib cage, arms and legs flailing like a June bug on its back, I oscillated between watching his bespectacled approach with fear and wariness and barking instructions like a drill sergeant.

"Remember to put it on thick! Check the clock before you start!"

Inches away from smearing my privates with toxic pink goo, he froze.

"I don't think I can." He looked neither deep into my eyes, nor deep anywhere, focusing instead somewhere over my left shoulder. "No," he concluded, "I definitely can't."

I lowered my legs and propped myself up on my elbows. "Yes, you can! You have to help me. The last time I tried it myself, I ended up looking like a trichinosis victim. And I nearly zapped off my magic button."

He looked forlorn now. "I can't. I'd never be able to look at you the same way again."

Heaving myself straight up, I snapped, "Of course you can. How do you think gynecologists do it? They have wives to go home to, you know."

"But you *are* my wife," he pleaded, putting down the paraphernalia like it was an active grenade. "I'm not supposed to know how you get beautiful; I'm supposed to just enjoy it. I'm certainly not supposed to take part in it."

"Oh, bull-tooties," I admonished, flopping back down. "Find me where it says *that* in the Good Book." My poor young Reverend husband loved me dearly, I knew, and I him, but nothing in seminary school prepared him for marrying a wife with a lifelong dream of lounging on a Caribbean beach wearing three of the teeniest triangles of red Lycra possible.

I had, however, since meeting and marrying him fourteen months previously, made my position repeatedly and crystal clear. "Fine, get out then or I'll smear some on you."

"Sorry, honey," he offered weakly before scuttling out the door. Shortly, I heard the TV click on and strains of cheering fans in some arena. Even preachers get to a point of needing a testosterone boost, I supposed.

Since it was his first congregation, we were as far into Creation as could support a church. It didn't help that our Volvo had recently died and due to the financial constraints of the imminent vacation, we'd opted to abandon Old Moses in the church parking lot until a (much) later date.

Consequently, the one shop in town that might have been able to fulfill my request was so old-fashioned it still called itself a "beauty parlour." There was no funky chrome and glass, only pressboard partitions. No techno-pop was pumped in from unseen speakers; only good old Joe Ramsey, local DJ extraordinaire, announcing Carpenters songs from the AM radio in the corner. Maeve cut and blow-dried—that is, stuck you under the big space-man hood; Josie permed and coloured, providing you wanted a blue afro, and Ginny swept and poured Nescafes. They were all over one hundred years old.

I sauntered in that afternoon and casually studied the board above the simple cash register, not having set foot in the place since they'd done my up-do for my high-school graduation dance. That was 1982, when I was a fresh-faced seventeen, and I still managed to look like Jackie Onassis on a very bad hair day. Ever since, I hacked away on my own and treated myself to a city cut whenever I was in one. Any city at all.

Needless to say, it was a pretty basic price-and-service list: cut and blow-dry, set and comb-out, colour rinse, perm, long hair and perm, short hair. Manicure had been added in felt pen at the bottom. Aaaah, I thought wickedly, somebody went on a course. God forbid the concept of acrylics be uttered in their presence. "Other services by request," also in spiky, felt-pen writing, caught my eye.

"Maeve," I tried nonchalantly, "what are these other services you gals provide, anyway?"

"Well, it's no kind of hanky-panky!" she answered vehemently.

That hadn't occurred to me, and I wish she hadn't brought it up. For weeks, I would carry around the vision of motley Josie in her Fortrel pantsuit, baby-oiling a towel-clad Mr. Peterson from the Chevron station.

"I'm sure it's not." I smiled brightly. "Just wondering what you've added to your vast repertoire of beauty regimes."

She narrowed her narrow eyes at me. "What are you looking

for, Deidre?" She obviously hadn't forgotten how I stormed out in tears without tipping her in June '82.

"I'm asking what you're offering, Maeve."

The drug lords of Columbia couldn't be cagier.

"We tweeze."

That sounded like a long and painful process, considering what I wanted tweezed.

"Tweeze?"

"Tweeze brows, dear."

I looked at hers—two pencilled-in squiggles of surprise—dubiously.

"What else?"

"We dilapidate unsightly hair."

Aaaah. Now we were getting somewhere.

"I think you mean depilate. But what do you depilate?" Sensing her answer would be unsightly hair, I quickly rephrased. "Where, where do you depilate?"

Her eyes were now mere slits. "Ladies' moustaches, of course. Where else?"

"Ladies' moustaches!" I repeated, disheartened. "Of course." I let a beat go by. "Do you wax?"

"Wax?"

"Wax. Legs. And such."

"And such?"

"DO YOU PERFORM BIKINI WAXES?" I exploded, suddenly not caring what the request did to my reputation as the Good Reverend's Wife.

". . . calling occcccccccupants of in-ter-pla-ne-tar-y, ex-tra-or-din-ar-y, craft . . ." crooned Karen C.

Maeve pursed her lips. "No. *We* don't do that type of thing here." Her lips then totally disappeared inside her face as she explained the salon's stance on such capital offences. "*We* don't have anyone who wishes to become that intimate with anyone, it being such a small town and all. *You* would have to go to the city." *. . . if you want to be violated by a depraved mind in such a way,* went unsaid.

"Okey-doke," I chirped, suddenly feeling my Levi's were made of Saran Wrap, my sweatshirt of loose mesh. "Just thought I'd check. Bye-bye now, Maeve." Giving a chaste nod to Josie and Ginny, who were peeking out from their respective cubicles, I backed out of their Mecca of propriety-in-beautification.

It was the Devil incarnate who said through Maeve's mouth, just before I was out of earshot, "See you in church on Sunday, Deidre. In that front pew for the Reverend's wife."

And so, my botched self-job, lack of wheels, the archaic salon, and my husband's squeamishness left me as cranky, not to mention woolly, as a bear in March. We were leaving for Bermuda in two days. I hadn't worked out and starved all winter to wear a sarong or bike shorts, or to stay wrapped in a towel with my knees pressed together. I was going where no Reverend's wife had gone before and I wanted to be little-red-bump-free to do it.

I wore my most pristine dress on Sunday morning, knowing the preacher's wife's wish to deface her God-given body would have spread through the three counties that arrived for services. It may have been my imagination, but it seemed the old biddies pursed, the mid-lifers looked on in bare tolerance, the young mums commiserated, and the older teens looked at me with a whole new respect—a respect I hadn't managed to draw out while leading the six-week Teen Crusaders course last fall. After the sermon, young Chelsea Durham sidled up to me.

"Mrs. Lithgow?" she whispered urgently. "Mrs. Lithgow! I need to talk to you."

Thinking she needed a chat about the ramifications of self-pleasuring, or perhaps that a boyfriend was responsible for one of the town's four unsolved crimes, I led her quickly into my husband's office.

From her Bible—somewhere between Leviticus and Deuteronomy, guessed my practised eyes—she pulled out a slip of paper.

"Here," she said conspiratorially. "It's the number for my cousin, Shelly. She's an esthetician in the city. She can do the job." Chelsea lowered her voice even more. "The job you need doing."

I studied her solemn eyes. "Ah, that's very kind of you to look into *the job* for me, Chelsea, but I'm afraid I don't really have enough time left. Joey Sykes is driving us to the city tomorrow afternoon, to an airport hotel, and the flight's the next morning."

"She's got her own shop. She'll open it up for you if need be; I already asked."

Suddenly, the number of people envisioning, in one way or another, my scalped or bushy . . . *bush*, was most disconcerting. "Chelsea, it was just, well, just so darn kind of you to look into this for me, but I'll just, um, take the Bic to my, er, to It."

"Gosh no, Mrs. Lithgow! You'll have little red bumps for days and then regrowth before your vacation's even over!"

I didn't know whether to hug her or demand that she burn all of her *Cosmopolitan* back-issues, the only readily available source of such information I could think of.

"I think it's really important, Mrs. Lithgow. All the girls do. We think you've just got an awesome body and you're pretty cool, too, for a Reverend's wife and well, you should do it for all of us stuck in this winter Hellhole. Heck-hole," she quickly corrected, flushing. "I'll call my cousin back and she'll come right to your hotel room."

I was speechless.

"It's okay; she'll do it no problem. She owes me because I'm the only one that knows why she went to Seattle so suddenly that summer."

I sighed, my forays into thong bikinis now utterly tame in comparison to what else went on behind closed doors.

"Well . . ."

"Do it, Mrs. Lithgow! Do it for all the young people who Maeve made look like those Golden Girl chicks for their first dates. Do it!"

"All right. All right! Make the call, Chelsea Lee. We'll be at the Ramada Airport Inn anytime after six tomorrow. I'll be waiting."

"With legs splaaaay . . ." she started in a singsong voice.

"Enough, Chelsea," I warned.

Chastened, she added authoritatively, "I'll tell her you want the Full Brazilian."

"The what?" I asked, feeling weak in the knees and vulnerable in the crotch.

"The Full Brazilian! It's like, the only way to go. One inch by two," she crowed knowledgeably, drawing the auspicious shape in the air.

"The Full Brazilian," I breathed, thinking about getting stoned by the Elders at some point down the road, if not for this, then something else. "Yes. The Full Brazilian it is!"

The Lord works in mysterious ways to bring our dreams about, indeed He does.

The Dog Park

"Ah, for Christ's sake, Chumley, stop rolling in the horse poop," I holler and start heading in his direction. He waits until I'm about ten feet away, indulges in one last wriggle, and takes off across the grass at a rate I have no desire, or ability, to even try to match. I take a moment to visualize my recently cleaned bathroom after ridding the hairy galoot of his latest stench.

"That'd be from the Mounted Police," growls Ol' Crazy beside me. "Like them cops are too important to scoop their own shit." He pats his dog, a balding, stuffed toy he named Madeinchina. He, or she, peeps out from the breast pocket of the pea jacket he wears 365 days a year. Ol' Crazy's harmless and loves real dogs too, so we don't mind him hanging around the dog park.

In case you're not into dogs, that's a city park where you run your condo-bound canine without a leash during certain hours (which not a lot of people pay attention to). It's a very communal, low-key atmosphere where the owners all stand around with nifty portable coffee cups, chatting about how cute each other's dogs are, watching out for mud or fertilizer-eating, violence, toy-hogging, injury, or humping. Occasionally we exchange other helpful dog-oriented tidbits. Chum, the most hilarious, best-looking, and friendly dog you could ever have, is a pound cross of Lab, St. Bernard, and something no vet has put a finger on yet. I admit it: it's like he's my son.

Here's an inside joke: how do dog owners know when it's time to grocery shop? Answer: when they run out of plastic bags.

Get it?

My boyfriend (his name's Parker and he's gorgeous in a mature, California surfer kind of way) and I both work full-time, so one of us takes out Chumley in the early morning and the other after work. It switches, depending on who went to bed later the previous night and what my restaurant shifts are. I've been known to get out of my shift by trading it for sex.

This day, I'm standing around talking to this woman, one eye on Chumley to make sure he doesn't bolt across the street after this cat that loves sitting in its bay window to torture him, and one eye on her. It's a drizzly weekday, so we're alone.

She's dang cute, making me painfully aware of the ball cap covering my unwashed, mouse-brown, sticky-outy hair and baggy jacket, filthy from being jumped on by, well, literally everybody's dog. (I always have cookies in my pockets.) My jeans—Parker's, truth told—are also mud-splattered. She, on the other hand, sports black stretch-pants, amazingly clean hiking boots, a snazzy Mountain Equipment Co-op anorak, a perky ponytail, and, *yeeeaaaaccccchhh*, makeup.

We're talking about how much time dogs take to properly care for, especially big ones, though she has a yappy little Sheltie. I cut her off to yank Chum away from a Great Dane he hates.

So now she confides, "Lucky me, I'm moving out to the 'burbs in a few weeks—North Burnaby. Bought a place with a big fenced yard, so it'll be great."

"You bought within five-hundred clicks of Vancouver? Impressive." Parker and I'll be renters in this city forever.

"I know! Crazy, real estate's crazy here. I had some success at work and can finally afford it."

Okay, I'll take the bait. She looks like a travel agent; maybe she got a sales award for selling the most Cancun getaways. No, she's probably IT. Everybody's IT these days. I say, "Great. What do you do?"

"I'm a writer. Fiction. Knopf picked up my new crime series."

Suddenly, I am torn between passionate love and dire hate for this woman, for I have a pile of rejection letters from every blinkin' publisher on the continent. Enough to wallpaper my office, if I were so inclined. If I had an office. Meanwhile, my unpublished historical romance keeps getting more historical and I get more hysterical. I refrain from telling her any of this; she might think I'm looking for an in, which I am.

"Woo-hoo," I say simply. "Knopf's big." Wait. A new series as in her debut, or new as in her tenth round of cadavers and detectives with different names?

She shrugs. I guess one can be nonchalant when one's already there.

"Kippy, honey, out of the mud!" she sings, and yippy-yappy Kippy trots over immediately. I guess, in all fairness, Kippy is kind of cute, but he's only about twenty pounds, max, so wouldn't be much fun to wrestle with or utilize as a footstool.

"Chumley," I call out rather feebly, knowing it will fall on (self-induced) deaf ears. Sure enough, he lifts his lug head just enough to say, "Get real!" before reburying his nose in some form of muck. I clear my throat. To call him again will only bring further attention to the fact that he has the capacity to be more insolent than a teenager. The trick is to time my verbal commands with his natural commencement of desired action.

"So, when's your book coming out?" I ask casually. Frickin' dickin'. I am totally jealous; I feel green-monster-goo filling my body.

"My latest series?" she clarifies subtly. "There's three to start. Anyway, it will be a couple of weeks."

I think of asking about the launch party, but that will look like I'm hinting for an invite or that I personally know something about publishing, which vicariously and theoretically I do, but I wouldn't want to be put to the test. Still, I'd love to hang at a trendy Yaletown bar, schmoozing wit' da local literati. "Cool. Did I say congratulations? What's your name again? I'll look out for you. I mean, your books."

"Thank you! I'd appreciate your support. I have a small but loyal, kind of cult following. I'm Tricia Richler."

Aha! She's related to Mordecai Richler. So that's her in.

"No relation to Mordecai," she says breezily, as if she's been accused of such nepotism before. "Anyway, I should go. Come on, Kippy. Let's go pack some more."

Is she miffed I didn't know her name right off?

Kippy looks deliriously happy at her suggestion. Chumley would only like it if he were in charge of cleaning out the fridge. I'm sure packing paper and boxes would freak him out; he won't even step over a silent vacuum to get a chunk of steak.

"Okay, see ya," I say to my new best, published-author friend. At that, Chumley bolts across the street and behind someone's house, which I'm sure Tricia notes. I stomp after him and feel perturbed.

"Tricia? With the little Sheltie?" Parker says when I tell him about my encounter. "Yeah, I've talked to her a few times."

"She didn't tell you about getting published? *Multiply* published?" I stress and give Chum a pretzel from the bowl in my lap because he's looking so (ha ha) starved and forlorn.

"Nah. We talk dogs; you know how it is."

Parker is rapidly flipping through our zillion channels. I wrest the clicker away from him and settle us on an episode of *Law and Order*. "I took an extra breakfast shift tomorrow, so you're on AM duty, okay?" He grunts his acceptance, and I snuggle into him.

We've been going out for four years now, living together for two. I love the comfort level of knowing someone this long. I love knowing to put extra salt and butter on his vegetables so they taste less vegetably. I *love* to find the mole above his left butt-cheek with my fingertips or tongue. I love his predictability, his solidity.

I work my breakfast shift at this sleazoid diner down the street from our apartment—I only like it because you can wear jeans and T-shirts—then come home to scroll through my 327-page work-in-progress. I revamp my query letter for the ninety-ninth time in hopes that the minute changes I make will be the changes that make some front-line Acquisitions Editor go, "Hey, Big Cheese Editor, I got a hottie here," and offer me a quarter-mil advance.

I realize I have to figure out better motivations for Belinda to go back to Charles after he killed her dog. The fact that he can undo her corset with one hand isn't enough.

I run the pooch around the block and change into my issued

red Polo and khakis for my oh-so-much-classier evening shift in a nearby funky Californian-style restaurant. It's great money—I usually bring home at least sixty bucks, frequently a hundred—and it's flexible enough that when I'm on a big writing jag, I can get my hours covered super easy. The downside is, I'm sick of rah-rahing potato skins, cheese sticks, and suicide wings. Even the once-exotic *baba ganoush* is now old hat.

It's 12:30 when I get home. Parker is asleep on the couch, but Chumley greets me at the door. I leash him up for his late-night bonus pee. My Ken doll is hauling himself off the couch when we skitter back in.

"Hi. How was your day?"

"Okay. Seventy bucks, no spilled dishes or ass-grabbing. Yours?"

"Newsy, actually. They want to transfer me out to the Burnaby branch, make me full manager, actually. The Burnaby shithead got fired for pilfering CDs." Parker's an assistant floor manager for A&B Sound.

"Well, yee-haw! Great but yuck, right? Commuting, how do you feel about that?" My mind leaps as we head to bed; maybe we can move to a cheaper place in the boonies, I can quit my jobs and write full-time . . .

He strips and attempts to three-point each article of clothing into the laundry basket. "I'll be going against the flow, on SkyTrain. They're giving me a small raise," he says and holds up a hand at the beginnings of my cheer, "which will just cover buying a transit pass."

I kiss him and say congratulations anyway. "Are you okay? You seem distracted."

Parker gives himself a shake before climbing into bed. "Huh? No, I'm good. Chum was a pain in the ass earlier though, totally disobedient. He needs to get out more, burn off more energy, you know?"

I nod in commiseration, willing someone to patent a gerbil wheel for dogs.

"Who was there, at the park?" I inquire, sliding in beside him.

He's drifting off already. Men! "Umm, Ken, you know the guy with the Shepherd, the woman with that big white poodle, a cou-pla' new ones. Kippy."

"Kippy the Wonder-dog and his master, Vancouver's answer to P.D. James?" I disguise the snippiness I feel.

"You sound snippy," confirms Parker, punching his pillow into place. Does the man know me or what?

"Sorry. I'm a tad jealous."

"She says you could give her your stuff to look over."

I bolt to a sitting position and snatch the pillow from under his head to wake him up. "You told her about me? Oh, gross. I'm not showing her anything."

He pulls the pillow back and resettles. "Suit yourself."

Suddenly, I am wide awake, irrationally pissed that Parker talked to this woman about me. I mean, she writes mysteries; I'm into nineteenth-century romances. What could she possibly tell me? "Like a thousand things," I grumble out loud.

"Huh? Anyway, I'll tell her thanks but no thanks, unless you want me to express your more exact sentiments."

"No," I pout. "I just want to do it my way."

"Okay, as long as you're prepared to waitress indefinitely," he cautions tiredly. "Or unless you want to do other stuff and just write for fun."

Whoa! This is a dangerous topic in broad daylight.

"You're saying you want me to get a real job," I embellish.

Parker doesn't answer.

I lie awake, frowning into the darkness, long after Parker has stopped twitching and flopping around. I have to get something published. Now.

The next day, my day off from both eateries, I skip the park in lieu of a long beach-walk with Chumley. He runs around in his spazzy way, but keeps coming back to check on me as I amble along. Dogs are so friggin' smart, the way they sense stuff. I mean, I'm okay, just a little melancholy and wondering whether I really should look for a real job. It wouldn't be for the money, that's for sure, but did I want to be twenty-nine and a waitress? Thirty-nine? Forty-nine?

I send out a couple more query letters of yesterday's zipped-up version, collect two please-fuck-off (AKA PFO) rejection slips from the mailbox, and improvise chicken parmesan for dinner. Usually, on my day off I do a grown-up dinner and the double dog-duty thing, but Parker sucks back the chicken like it's one long piece of spaghetti and insists on taking out Chum.

"Why don't you use the time to write?" he suggests, when I offer to come.

I force myself to smile gratefully, though I'm not sure whether I want to take his words as pressure or support.

They leave and I sit in front of a blank Word screen for a full minute, minute and a half, before giving up and flopping down on the couch with the remote. Not that I think a Seinfeld rerun is going to inspire me, but you never know.

When I hear his key in the lock—three whole hours later!— I scramble back to the computer and start wildly banging out this insipid idea about a woman waiting at a bus stop, which I've had in my head for months.

"Hi!" I say with false bravado when he finally approaches me with a bland kiss on the cheek. "Yowsa, three hours. Chummie must be in his glory."

"Yeah," he moves off. "Actually, it wasn't really three hours of playing. A couple of us hit Starbucks for an hour."

"I hope you bought Chum decaf or we'll be up all night entertaining him," I quip.

"Uh-huh," he says, like it's a real consideration.

I consider getting up and thwacking him, but I committed to at least writing an outline, so I ignore his weirdness.

Parker drifts off to bed; I write for another two hours, then take Chum up for a rooftop pee. He does nothing but I wanted to make sure because I don't like my Saturday mornings disturbed.

Not that I had to worry. Sometime before eight, I wake up enough to squint at the clock and simultaneously register that neither Parker nor Chumley are in the condo. It feels good to sink back into a dreamy state, though I can't help but think how bloody indebted I'm going to be, as far as walks go. Or sex.

My boys saunter in around ten-thirty. Actually, Parker *swaggers* and Chumley galumphs.

"Hey, you were energetic. What time did you guys leave?"

"Not sure. What time did you wake up? Hey! I bought bagels. D'ya want me to toast you one?"

Over the next two weeks, I don't dog-walk much, but I do put out a lot because Parker's in quite the horny phase. Since sex takes a lot less time and energy than running Chumley, not to mention that you don't get as dirty and sweaty, I figure I have the good end of the deal.

I begin to suspect a mislaid generosity when I clean out the pockets of his dog-walking coat before it hits the washer and I find all the receipts. I smell a rat. Or many double mocha lattes, as the receipts reflect.

I confront Parker after work when he starts hunting for his jacket.

"So, Parker," I say glibly, "guess what I found today?"

Unfortunately, he isn't looking at me, so I can't see if he assumes a guilty expression or not. "Parker?"

"I don't know, Cari. A publisher?"

That's low, and it stings, but I make a goofy face at his back to blow out the poison. "Very funny, but alas, no. I found, like, seven receipts from Starbucks. What's up?"

He blanches, then flushes. "Well, I . . ."

"Yeah," I conclude sanguinely. "You're busted. A., Chummie isn't quite getting the hours of exercise it seems and B., I thought we were reserving coffees out for very special occasions only and putting said formerly peed-out monies into the house account. It was your idea, after all."

Now he turns green.

"Quite the Technicolor display you've put on here for us tonight, Mr. Caffeine Addict and blatant House-Fund Sucker-Outer." I punch him in the arm, somewhere between playful and for real, and stalk into the kitchen in a theatrical huff. I personally haven't had a fancy coffee for several months. I guess the restaurant jobs keep me from cheating.

Parker has a six-thirty AM breakfast meeting in North Vancouver a few days later, so I take Chumley out around nine. (This would be one of those not-off-leash times, according to the sign, but since I often scoop foreign poop, I claim immunity.)

The old man with the two white powder-puffs is there.

Chumley bounds up to them like always, then they settle into their usual sniff-figure-eight, sniff-figure-eight routine. From the other end of the field, I see Authoress Extraordinaire and Yappy. Kippy. She's wearing a tam, her hair's down, and it's as fluffy as the two Terriers.

"Hi!" I say cheerily, flipping up my ball cap a notch so I don't look like such a derelict. "It's Cari and Chumley. We met once before?"

In turn, Madam Grisham zips up the stand-up collar of her anorak and tilts her chin down so I can only see her eyes and half her nose. "I remember."

From the complete, complete other side of the field, Chumley bounds full-speed, like we're some kind of unmanned hot-dog stand. He lurches to a halt at Tricia's feet, his tail wagging so hard that I think he may take flight. She takes an expensive-looking treat from a little baggie in her breast pocket.

This woman, he likes.

I watch her lyrically command him to sit, woof, shake a paw, stuff I'd taught him over the last year.

She high-fives with him. Last week's trick.

This woman, he knows.

This woman knows him.

Something's rotten in the state of Denmark, and it ain't uncollected turds.

The three of us—seven, if you count the dogs—shunt around for twenty minutes before the white fluffs are hustled off into the burgundy sedan in which they always arrive.

The park suddenly seems too big and too small at the same time.

"Let's go for coffee," I suggest.

"Oh, I can't. I'm supposed to be proofing some galleys; that's when the writer—"

I hold up a hand. "I know what galleys are." My haughty voice surprises me.

She nods slowly. "Right. Your boyfriend, what's his name? Paul? Parker. Right, Parker says you're working really hard at getting published too. Hang in there. I had to go through, gosh, five or six rejections before I got picked up."

I imagine her getting pelted with hundreds of deflated, slobbery dog-park balls.

"Yes, well, I am nothing, if not patient," I smile brightly. Like a fucking blinding eclipse, I hope. "Come on, let's have a quickie. Coffee." I take a measured step toward her and she takes a step back. Apparently, I look pretty big and tough, all uncosmeticked and all.

"Well, okay, but my treat."

You've got *that* right, toots.

"Kippy, come."

The damn rat comes bouncing right up, sits primly at Tricia's left heel, and stretches up his scrawny little neck to facilitate being leashed for the three-block walk to Starbucks. I wish the annoying little moppet great ill. Nothing drastic, like an incident with a chicken bone; more like an all-night, in-house diarrhea session. Something more damaging to owner than dog.

After five minutes (which is a long time when you're being watched) of me rounding up Chumley, we set off. We talk dog the whole way, which, under the circumstances, is our only safe topic.

Then, having secured the pooches to the wrought-iron fence around a Starbucks tree, we move inside and join the perpetual line. I steal a glance at the wanna-be-but-Cari-hopes-never-gonna-be

Giller Prize-winner. She looks pinched, a most unflattering look.

Still, I am encouraged by the aura of familiarity between she and El Barrista (fancy way of saying coffee guy).

"Hey, Tricia," says Leon, minimum-wage shift supervisor. "The usual?" He's everything I'd hoped for and a teeny bit more. She nods spasmodically and shunts toward the cash register. Leon, minimum-wage shift supervisor, adds, "Boyfriend working today?"

Wisely, Tricia ignores him, pays for her coffee only, and scuttles away to an outdoor table. To be closer to the dogs? More like to be farther away from Leon, the documentarian of her caffeine history.

It's my turn. "Grande latte with a shot of Amaretto, please." Then I lean in to conspire. "Are they still together? I thought they broke up."

"Oh, I couldn't!" says Leon, all coquettish, but dying to spill, I can tell.

Who needs Sugar Twin when there's sweet Leon? I offer him a woeful smile. "It's just that, I won't bring him up if . . ."

Leon nods in a commiserating way. "I'm positive they're still together. You mean the tall blond guy, with a moustache? I think his name's Paul. They seemed pretty couply, if you know what I mean, just last night. He's cute. For a het."

I slam down a fiver with a ferocity that makes Leon jump and slosh the syrup shot.

"You pay down there, at the till," he informs, recovering.

"What time last night?" I press, perceiving that my coy Colombo days are finished.

I must look authoritative, because he answers, "Around eleven? Twelve? We're short a supervisor, and I'm a little tired from doing lots of back-to-back shifts."

Parker had insisted that three extra-strength Tylenol and a Neo Citran packet at ten would knock me out enough to scare off a niggling cold. I was too doped register to any coming and going.

Suddenly, I can't play-act anymore. I guess I give Leon some harsh or revealing look, because he gulps and abandons me for the next customer. I pay and stride to our table under the awning, which spares us from the incessant rain.

"Ho-ho. So. What do you want?" I ask Tricia like a dip.

She smiles nervously (*I* think), and pretends I'm talking to Chum, who pushes at me in his usual depraved manner.

"I'm talking to you, Tricia," I say when both dogs have been placated with pats and the cookie remnants from my pockets. "What the hell do you want from my Parker?"

She nods, sagely, like she's some therapist, acknowledging profundity, but not curtailing it.

Chumley pees against the plastic leg of the next table.

"I love him," she says quietly.

"You barely know him," I counter.

"Long enough to know," she says smugly. She sips and adjusts her beret. "I'm just being honest."

Chumley, who is tall enough, plunks his head on the table. Like me, Tricia reaches out to caress him and our fingers touch in his mane for half an electrifying second before we snatch back our hands.

"And he has told you he feels . . . what? Honestly."

"He loves me, too."

Now, instead of green-monster-goo, I am filled with yellow bile.

"This is insane," I choke out and lob my $3.57 coffee into the garbage can to my left. Three points. Then I am pissed at my impulsiveness, knowing how many specialty coffees Parker's sucked back recently, among other things.

I breathe and continue. "I've known him for four years. You just met him. This is insane," I repeat, but with different emphasis.

"Maybe," she agrees, standing. "Look, you talk to him and you guys figure it out."

"That's really goddamn noble of you." I can't stand her saccharine calm.

But she blows that image when she leans into me and adds evilly, "You misinterpreted, Cari. I meant, go confirm the strength of his feelings toward me. We're utterly committed. Why would I have told you so easily? Parker and I have already discussed it."

I will my discarded coffee to rise out of the bin and explode in her face.

It doesn't.

We part on closed, guarded terms, and I deliberately head in a different direction than she. The detour makes me late for work and I get reprimanded. I want to lip-off the weenie little manager, three or four years my junior, but sense kicks in at the last nano second because I realize I will really need this job. I mutter an apology and launch into a barely intelligible diatribe about womanly troubles. As I suspected, he cannot handle this and shooshes me on to the lunch hostess to get my section assigned.

I'm off at nine. I consider going out to a club to get tanked and picked up. Since I don't drink and there's no guarantee of the latter—the reality of which would send me over the Lions Gate Bridge—I just go home.

Parker is sitting on the beanbag chair in the dark and I almost sit on him, having sought velvety blackness myself.

"Shit!" I accuse, wiggling my ass off his left leg. "I almost sat on you." We settle into ironically close positions and sit in silence for a few minutes. Obviously, Tricia has spoken with him or at least left some warped message via the various modern means of communication to the effect of: *She knows; prepare yourself.*

My opening contribution?

"Your breath smells like cunt."

He bolts out of the beanbag. "Jesus, Cari! Don't talk like that!"

I don't know what possessed me. Of course the C-word is banned in our home. Still, I'm perversely pleased at the response it evokes, even though it's at my entire gender's expense.

I try to sound casual. "Hey, I think it's admirable that you can get it up within nine hours of your four-year girlfriend finding out what a cheating bastard you are."

I watch his pacing silhouette against the cloth blinds.

"Just go," I say. "Go by tomorrow night when I get back from work. Leave the CDs, linen, dishes, furniture . . . leave every fucking thing except your clothes and the stupid Harley poster." He stops pacing and inhales deeply, like you do when you've truly forgotten to breathe.

"It just happened. I don't know how. I didn't mean . . ."

"To hurt me," I finish for him sarcastically. "Classic. One question: it's true? You're committed?"

"I love her. It started . . ."

"Stop! Not another word. I don't want a single detail. Just shut up."

"I want Chummie."

I leap up as if a retractable leash has dictated my movement.

"We'll have a yard, and it backs onto a creek and greenbelt." His hands are behind his head and his elbows protrude like devil horns.

"Never. Never! He was my idea. He's *my* dog!"

We're both shouting.

"That's bullshit! He's *our* dog and when we split, he should go with who can provide best."

"Try it," I hiss.

The devil horns collapse.

"Cari, think about it. You'll never be able to run him enough alone. This way, he gets all day to run and swim in the creek. There's also a dog park, two blocks away, so he can still socialize."

I grab a whimpering Chumley by the collar and drag him into the bedroom, prodding him onto the same bed that his previous attempts to infiltrate have resulted in smacks to his haunches. I've locked the bedroom door and I lie down, my face buried into the folds of his furry neck and jowls. Chumley, in his infinite wisdom, puts up with me.

Both are not leaving me; this much I know.

It actually happens as fast as I had demanded. When I come home from work, the closets, dresser, shoe rack, and bedroom wall have gaping holes. I shift my stuff around, but the illusion fools no one. I take out Chum and stand apart from the others, crying and waiting for him to sniff, pee, poop, run, and wrestle himself into delirium, sad I can't do the same. An elderly woman with a Springer Spaniel comes over to me and pats my back.

"It'll be okay, dear. He'll come to his senses, or you'll come to yours. Either way, you'll be okay."

I gulp and hiccup and stare at her, wishing just this once for rain so the drops would cover my tears. "You knew?"

"A guess. Old ladies like me can be real flies on the wall, or on the park bench."

I look skyward and she moves away. Except for Ol' Crazy, who waggles Madeinchina at me, they all leave me alone. Even the dogs.

The next few weeks are a total blur. Parker calls a few times, to make sure I'm okay and to see if I want to talk, but I keep hanging up on him. After five or six tries, he stops. Chumley takes to peeing in the closet and if I had money, I'd take him to one of the new fangled dog therapists. Plus, we both put on weight as lack of time and especially spirit result in us sharing the couch more than is ideal.

Parker had left Tricia's address and phone number in case of emergency (but not crisis), and one day after about four weeks, I get my friend Joy to drive me out there.

It's a boring, 1970s house, but fenced and surrounded by trees, just like Parker said. Chumley strains his head out the back window, sniffing and looking as we sit in the idling car across the street from my guy's new life.

I know what I should probably do, but instead I just swear to get out more. I bundle up my manuscript and put it in a trunk. The short story about the lady at the bus stop spurs me to write another and another and pretty soon I have, like, eight. Some of them are even funny, though heartache seems to be the prevailing theme.

When one of them is bought by *Bathtub Gin*—payment being one contributor's copy—Chumley and I celebrate by buying him a new collar, followed with a four-hour hoof around the Seawall. Our mutual couch-fat has stabilized, but not dissipated.

I agree to meet Parker in a Wal-Mart parking lot. It's been four months. I bring his CDs, Hibachi, and a quilt his grandmother crocheted, knowing it's not enough.

"I still really think Chumley belongs with me," he says after sucky salutations.

To my horror, I start crying. "You can't have him. We've worked it out."

"Cari, I'm sure you need him as company, but think of what I can offer."

"You can't get the new girl and the old dog, Parker! It's not fair!" I shout, pounding him on the thigh.

He catches my wrist. "You're being selfish!"

"*Me* selfish? What the hell are you then, jumping ship, beds, like that, for no reason, with no warning?"

He releases my wrist and puts his hands on the steering wheel. "I have no defence to that. I was hugely selfish but I am also extremely happy. Besides, you're not giving up Chummie for me; you'd be doing it for him."

"Well, it feels like it would be another bonus for you," I snap, opening the door and sticking a foot out, readying for flight. I don't want this conversation, this knowledge of his new life, after all.

"Think about it. You know where to find us."

I borrow Joy's rattle-trap and take Chumley out to North Burnaby three weekends later without calling first. I bang on the front door. When Parker comes to the door, I say nothing—couldn't, even if I wanted to; my throat's burning so bad. Feeling like a macabre Marcel Morceau, I lead Parker back to the sidewalk where I've dumped all the dog junk. I hand over Chum, bathed and brushed and on his leash.

I can only drive around the corner before breaking into hysterics that wrack my whole body, convulsions so big they shake the car. I think about what deciding custody of a kid must be like.

Something to Justify the Day

Mary, Mary, quite contrary, how do your fingernails grow?

Virginia has never been very particular putting on nail polish, going through the whole rigamarole of soaking her cuticles, buffing, and base-coating. Today, gloopy Burnished Red is going on over chipped Berry Burgundy. She feels a bit cheap painting her toenails out there on the front stoop, for all the world to see, and looking like a contortionist as she strains to reach her baby toes. It is, however, the first of May and she feels duty-bound to gulp in copious amounts of spring.

She does her fingernails too. Usually she forgets about the whole procedure because the paraphernalia is way under the bathroom sink in the Tupperware container—the container whose lid she had wrecked by laying it on a medium-high element. By the time she pulled it off, the plastic lid resembled bubble gum after drinking something hot. It was quite a shame, but it was funny, too. She had found it funnier than he.

They are wretched things, her fingernails—bitten down to the quick, the cuticles bloody at worst, inflamed and tender at best. He grabs a thumb or finger every once in a while, having seen a flash of angry, red skin, and examines it. She quickly yanks her hand back, silently chastised. Once, when she was feeling particularly petulant, she had put the argument back to him. *Maybe if you had an ounce of romance, and painted them for me, or presented me with a $1.79 bottle of Cutex in a colour of your choice, I would try harder.*

Nice example of taking responsibility, she knows.

Anyway, making a deal with him was setting herself up for failure.

Again.

God does not deal, and only fools make deals with the Devil.

Maybe her hands should be bound behind her back for a period.

Nibble gnaw nibble gnaw, no hurrah.

Still, from a distance, the twenty clumpy squares of colour will be something to show him, her husband of eight months, when she picks him up at the bus stop. "See, honey? She what I did today?" she will say in her baby voice and he will respond, "Oh, nice."

He will be grateful she is not showing him another Thumb. The right. She examines it now. Three-quarters grown in. The thumb she had gouged at with tweezers and teeny scissors until she damaged the root so badly, she had to tell people she had slammed it in a door. He had visibly squirmed when she cited it as yet another example of her self-destructive behaviour.

While out on the cedar-stained porch, she carefully plucks up the spiral notebook and pen beside her, the latter feeling awkward, since her world used to be ruled by computers. The salesman had said this would happen—that at first she would want to hand-write her drafts, but eventually she'd draw blanks without a key-board. These days she could not write, could not scrawl, as fast as her thoughts came. She needed to get those voices out before they destroyed her.

And she is thinking fast today, too fast for even the computer. It is supposed to be a letter but has turned into disjointed scrawl-ing blurbs and doodles.

Helter Skelter.

She thinks about dinner. They had eaten chops last night, which meant he had taken chops for lunch, in Tupperware that had been spared its lid. Seven-dollar Tupperware containers bought only because it was a friend's party.

Waste-smaste.

Can she Shake 'n Bake over top of the pre-baked, teriyaki-sauced leftover chops? It would be like eating shoes, she decides, and he will want something barbequed anyway, since it is sunny. She lopes into the house on her heels to save the carpet from streaks of Burnished Red, a stain even harder to remove than blood. Virginia sifts through the freezer, pulls out a frozen block of hamburger, and leaves it zapping on defrost in the microwave, cursing herself for not accomplishing this one small task earlier and for wrecking three nails.

Returning to the front porch, where the afternoon sun hits best, Virginia sits on the first of four wooden steps to the lawn. She is wearing jean cut-offs. They are too tight. Not in the waist or butt—across the legs. It is grotesque, the way the material bites into the flesh of her thighs, squishing them out, binding them like elas-tic bands around a pillow. Several minutes had been spent in front of the mirror, poking and pulling at the fleshy spillover to no avail.

Virginia remembers being seventeen and twenty-five pounds heavier and her sister slyly commenting that she looked better nude than in clothes. Now, over a decade later and twenty-five pounds lighter, she looks better *in* clothes than out. Too much skin had been leftover, so she resembled a Shar-Pei dog. Good thing there would be no babies, or she would really be a revolting bedroom spectacle. Twenty-five double handfuls of fat and muscle and other important inside stuff lost in as many days.

Gone gone gone, she's been gone so long . . .

All thanks to one of the quackier doctors and his quacky pills.

Anyway, it feels nice to be decadent like this, outside in shorts (if she did not look down) when everyone else she knows can only gaze at the milky sunshine from office windows. She had taken off her bra, *Flashdance*-style—it was now lying on the floor in the bathroom—from under the white, scoop-necked bodysuit that makes her feel thin and show-offy. Virginia has not felt show-offy in a long time. She tried to, downtown at the pub the other weekend when he was away playing rugby, but for some reason she just kept ducking her head from admiring glances.

At first, Virginia thought her avoidance was because she was now a virtuous married woman; then she just felt like she had completely lost it.

Lost in Spa-a-a-a-a-a-ce.

Anyway, she knows her nipples are visible through the white cotton (she checked), and it is kind of a miracle because she has pathetic nipples that are light and unresponsive. She wonders if they are visible from the street. No, that is silly. Besides, there are only women and their preschool children going by, and she has no desire to appeal to either of them.

One sauntering woman with a stroller had smiled and said hi. In return, Virginia smiled quickly and said hi, too. But the hi didn't come out very loud and she worried the woman had not heard her and now thought her a snob.

The slutty one, on the corner. Could not even say hello.

She makes sure the next one, with a stroller and a dog, gets an enthusiastic hello. Virginia truly does not want to appear stuck-up, does not want to be that show-off in the white bodysuit with her childless body intact—to the naked eye only—perched on her stoop, drinking rye and water, free of pot-bellied husbands and sneezing six-year-olds. Be nice, she instructs herself. Her husband, after all, will have to continue living among these people.

She could flirt with the Dickee-Dee man; he is safe enough. He is coming now; she can hear his distinctive, repetitive jingle.

Oh.

Yuck.

He is young and pimply and skinny and scuzzy.

What else would he be?

Why does he wear those big, black leather high-tops? He looks like a spindly little stick with big, clunky, orthopaedic shoes. She wonders briefly how he would be in bed. Virginia has not slept with anyone skinny and sinewy since she lost the weight. Lost half of herself.

It had always been most distressing to be in the position of screwing a skinny man, because she felt stronger and as though her pendulous breasts and Buddha stomach could easily smother her prey. In fact, she dumped one Skinny after a few dates when he hugged her and she felt panicked by his protruding ribs and bony shoulder blades. Davis. Well, that and he had asked if his level of education intimidated her. He was only a lawyer.

Pompous ass.

She found someone way better. Wonderful. Perfect. Her exact opposite, granted, but at the time it seemed a reasonable thing to want, because would he not balance her out?

It worked for a while. For a while, it seemed like he had the magic potion to lift the fog, but just when she had started to believe It would never come back, It did. Worse than ever. By that time they were married, and Virginia knows he feels that she trapped him, because he doesn't understand the fog or the anger and they can't find their perfect balance again. He keeps trying and she loves him for that, and on the days she is feeling very sad, she promises to keep trying to be happy, but he is less and less cheered and convinced by this promise every time he hears it.

I never promised you a rose garden . . .

Quitting that job was supposed to have made her happy. It sort of did. The thought of never having to go into that Barrington Street office again and face those people made her partly ecstatic, but she did not get happy *all over.*

Then there was the business idea. She was glad she used her personal pension money and nothing of their mutual funds, though they both know he still gets ripped off in the long run.

Every day she thinks about how she failed to make that business work. Every day. Especially now, when she is wallowing in the last bits of it. A few more straggly people to contact and tell them that there is no more business, a few leftover bits to gather from the rented suite on Kempt.

The business's slow death is both nauseating and numbing.

He thinks it is that she is lazy. Is she? It just feels like she hated it. Hated making those cold calls. Hated sitting alone all day, waiting for the phone to ring. When the phone did ring, it was usually some big company like Telus, wanting to know if she desired cellular phone service. A cellular? What the hell would she have done with a cellular? Only eight times in two months had it been someone with an interest in image consulting.

She spilled out her frustrations and fears late one night, and he said he understood, that he was not disappointed in her, but weeks later, he admitted he actually was. So for a while, Virginia oscillated between trying to make it work because it would make him proud and praying for it all to just wash away without her having to face it again.

Like bubbles down the drain.

The third thing is the book. It is done—the first draft, anyway—and he has read it and said it is good. They were lying in bed—not after making love or anything: she is always tired, angry, numb, or frozen. Virginia remembers the wave of fear that passed over her when he said into the dark, *Honey, about the book . . .* She had tensed because she thought he was going to shit on it and then she would lie there all night, eyes stuck wide open, mulling, mulling, while he slept, oblivious, as often happened for a variety of reasons.

But he had said it was good. It was just too short.

Then, after she spent a few days unproductively reading trashy library mystery novels, he accused her of letting yet another project slide. He was disappointed.

Again.

She tried to explain that she could not bear looking at the grainy printed pages right away, that she needed a few days to reflect and then she would tackle it again. He said, *Oh, I see.*

But he did not.

She knows it is unfair to expect him to be omniscient while

she feels ignorant of the simplest answer, but she continues to hope.

When she *had* done another draft, just last week, actually, he rallied and wasn't even mad that she still had not cleaned out the spare bedroom. He said, *I just like you to keep busy.*

No use explaining that her head is always frenetically busy, even when her body is immobile.

Virginia wonders what will come of those 67,419 words. It will sit in its old school binder forever because the concept of sub-mitting it is just too overwhelming. It is probably crap anyway.

Ding! she says out loud, practically feeling several facts collide within her skull. She hadn't really ever believed, not deep down, that the business would succeed either. Not really. Or that she would ever make him happy.

That she will ever be happy.

Virginia recalls relating to the woman in one of the psy-chotherapy groups who said, *I have never been happy, so how do I know what it feels like?* But that woman had been raped and molested and a whole bunch of other stuff, so it was understandable that she ask. Virginia, on the other hand, has been afforded every opportunity to *Get It Together* and still can not pinpoint a good reason to be so whacked. It made her sense of futility even more shameful.

Granted, she used to daydream about successes of all kinds: books published, Oscar nominations, and year-long trips around the world. Now, she cannot summon the energy to daydream, let alone find the motivation to *do*.

He thinks *doing* is the key. She tries to explain that she has to feel first, and *do* after.

He says she has it backwards, and this perpetual riddle confus-es her greatly. If she *did, did, did*, would she feel the right things? And how come the right feelings do not come from just *being*?

Lately, she starts feeling one thing, tries to explain it, and ends up feeling crushed and stupid, so she has come to not trust any of the feelings.

The neighbours are home now and they smile and wave from their driveway. They lean over their flower garden in front of their deck, exactly like hers, like the whole street's, to *ooh* and *aaah*. When they go inside, Virginia wonders if they are going to have a quickie before dinner, reasoning that one never knows what happens behind smiles and closed doors. Maybe they go in quickly because Wifey always gets a crack across the jaw at this time of day. Maybe Wifey has to take medication to keep from turning into a pumpkin.

Regardless, the neighbours' arrival spurs Virginia into action. It is 5:30, getting chilly and time to go pick him up at the bus exchange. (She does not like to be stuck at home all day without a car, even though there is nowhere to go that makes any difference.)

Virginia literally runs through the house, through each room, checking for loose items, disarray. The spare room is still in upheaval and he is right to be mad because it is mostly her stuff.

Shit.

Shoulda, coulda, woulda.

The chunky salad and the painted nails will have to do. Will they suffice? No. More fluff-stuff is required, so on the way to the bus exchange, she buys ice cream at the 7-Eleven. It is twice as expensive as Superstore's, but she doesn't have time to go all the way in to that tangled consortium. If she picks off the price tag, he won't know, and three more bucks will not make a difference now. Purchasing ice cream allows her to feel like a better wife. Fleetingly.

For about as long as she can hold a spoonful of it in her mouth without swallowing.

And dammit, she *is* a good wife in front of the colleague who joins them for drop-off, making up funny anecdotes about the day and her fundraising idea for Big Brothers Big Sisters and announcing they shall barbeque.

We barbequed all winter. He was fabulous. This poor husband of mine braved the elements for barbequed steak in February. What a scream!

The colleague is envious.

Virginia is a bit worried because she is tipsy from the rye and it is difficult to be gay and frivolous *and* tipsy *and* fakey happy *and* drive sensibly, all at the same time. When they drop the colleague off, she relaxes a little. Tenses and relaxes at the same time, actually, because the need for pretence is gone but she doesn't want to fight today.

Not today.

No matter how many times they do, she is always caught off-guard.

Wham!

He goes straight for the newspaper when they get home. While the patties grill and the broccoli steams, she stares at the back of the paper and wills him to lower it.

Fuck the teachers' strike. Fuck Israel. Take me in your arms and tell me it will be all right. One more time. If I heard it just one more time . . .

But he does not, and deep down, she knows he is unaware that she is staring. Still, Virginia says nothing, believing that it does not count if she has to ask for it.

Mary, Mary, quite contrary, how do your feelings grow?

Virginia leaves him to his dinner of burgers on bread topped with incongruous hunks of his stinky cheese, thickly sliced tomatoes, and instructions about the ice cream.

Before escaping, she kisses him tenderly on the forehead, then lips, to which he gives an abstracted grunt. She also whispers *I love you* and her voice cracks. She receives a slightly quizzical *love you too*, as expected. Then she goes upstairs without dinner, because she wants a flat stomach for the bath.

First she tidies up their bedroom, carefully smoothing the quilt and putting away his work clothes. On the dresser sits the framed, opening paragraph of "The Vine." Tennessee Williams. She presented it on their wedding night, in hopes he would feel like that someday—that he would yearn like the man in the poem, who reaches for his woman in the middle of the night, sensing she has left the bed, and feels utterly lost without her beside him.

Will he reach for her tonight?

In the bathroom, Virginia carefully locks the door, assembles everything necessary for the soak, and then lines them up satisfactorily along the rim of the tub.

Loofah. Shampoo. Deep conditioner. Apricot facial scrub.

Scented candle.

Five ounces of straight rye in a crystal wedding glass. Chipped already.

The saved-up prescriptions.

His straight razor.

It is hot and steamy and slippery in the tub.

She chastises herself again for having wasted so much time today.

Again.

Forgive me for wasting the day.

Virginia picks up the loofah and begins to scrub.

The Good Ear

For starters, it'd been difficult to get away. Two hundred and thirty-seven Croatian refugees needed direction about living space, grocery stores, and job postings. Of course, they weren't all physically at the Davie Street Welcome Society, but Deanne and her volunteer crew were deep into coordinating the logistics of settling the lot of them into their new Vancouver lives.

"Girl, you to be getting on that five o'clock ferry, if I recall," reminded Laticia, her boss, who looked like Nel Carter and operated her centre like Mother Teresa. Fortunately, Deanne's relationship with Laticia's younger sister hadn't spoiled their camaraderie at work.

"Yeah, yeah," Deanne had responded. "I really want to finish this daycare list first."

"S'not as important as your Granny's one-hundreth birthday. Get yourself out right now."

In the end, she caught the seven o'clock ferry to the Island, making her late for dinner, but at least not The Party, the 100th Birthday for forty-five people the next day.

"Hi," she dumped her tote bag inside the door of her aunt's kitchen. "Sorry, I missed the first . . . two ferries I meant to catch." She allowed the baby-bear hug from her Uncle Roger, her nose twitching from the cloud of Southern Comfort and Irish Spring soap that constantly clung to him. From Dave, newly divorced son of Aunt Linda, there was a grunted exchange. Deanne couldn't understand what dainty Chloe had seen in him, except maybe a lot of money from his trucking business. There was a chaste kiss on the cheek for Aunt Linda, a rakish woman whose perennially permed hair seemed even more tightly wound than usual, a springy helmet of sorts.

The family was three-quarters through dinner. Those who were having seconds were just gearing up; those who'd taken too much already were starting to push the remains about their plate and sigh about the injustice of such delicious food and so little stomach space.

"Hello, darling!" exclaimed Selma, her mother, rising from the table. They hugged, then Selma held her daughter at arm's-length.

The Survey.

She patted a portion of Deanne's dark, shaggy mane. "It's so wild," Selma mused, trying to sound upbeat, but not even coming close to controlling her unspoken yearning for a neat bob, a classic chignon. For her part, Selma wore the same style she had for years, a chic mushroom cap, Miss Clairol'd a shade or two darker this time, for variety.

"And oh dear," she continued, "you've spilled something on

your pretty skirt." They both peered at the light-red circle. And she didn't mean "pretty," or even wildly bohemian. She meant decidedly crumpled and second-handish. "It's ketchup," Deanne stated and extracted herself.

"Grandmom! It's me! How does it feel to be five hours away from a century?" She spoke into the left ear, the functioning one, while caressing the old woman's bony shoulders.

"Dee! Dee. Good Dee." The words were laborious, squeezing out of the left side of her mouth like a dripping faucet. It had been unrealistic to even hope that at ninety-eight, Agatha Booth would recover from a stroke, but they had.

Linda pulled a foil-covered plate out of the oven and placed it on the kitchen island. "It's probably very dry and I'm sorry, but you'll have to stand; the extra chairs are already placed in the living room. Or, you could eat in the den . . ." she trailed off. Linda Biggs did not want Deanne to eat in the den, any more than she desired her to crayon the walls.

"This is fine," assured Deanne, scraping off her portion of chicken wings onto an abandoned side plate.

"No chicken anymore? Well, for heaven's sake, I wish you'd told me. You can't just have vegetables. Look at that plate. Selma," she admonished, "look at that plate. If she'd only told me!"

"Please. Don't worry about it, but do you have any whole-grain bread?"

"Sixty percent," offered Uncle Roger, his tiny, baby-bird mouth full of mashed potatoes.

"Have some cheese at least. I've a block of cheddar, second shelf."

"Actually, I don't . . ."

"No cheese?"

"No animal products. Vegan."

"No wonder you look sick. You're probably anemic. All you supposedly health-conscious people are." Linda reached for her cigarettes and wine.

"I'm not anemic. The recommended grams of necessary protein are about half of what meat-eaters consume. Even vegans easily eat more protein than a body . . ."

"Give me a steak any day," piped in Dave, her cousin, well into his second plate. He smacked his lips and whacked a belly that dangled like an udder when he leaned over. "Fresh off the barbeque, still a little bloody when you make that first cut; are ya grossed out, Deanne?"

"Slightly, but it's got nothing to do with meat." She smiled falsely.

And they wondered how *she* had evolved from the same genes? She inwardly winced, imagining the imminent day when she'd announce she was gay and in love with Laticia's cousin.

After dinner, everyone settled in the TV room except Uncle Roger, who disappeared to obsess over the Home Shopping Network and glug Southern Comfort and apple juice from the Thermos under his bed.

"Don't you dare buy another porcelain doll for that brat next door," Linda barked at his back.

Deanne supported her grandmother's shuffle into the living room, a room more sacred than a sanctuary, yet far less private than a confessional. She positioned herself close to the good ear.

While caressing the old woman's hands, she gazed in awe at what the liver spots, scars, wrinkles, and bent fingers represented. Agatha, born in Perth, Scotland, arrived in Canada as a war bride and had more knowledge of life and death and everything in between than the rest of the family put together. Deanne thought it heart-wrenching that all her knowledge should now be locked up inside her.

Agatha's fingers were uncharacteristically unadorned. "Where's your ring? Where's your ruby ring?" she queried slowly.

Her grandmother looked with unseeing eyes at their inter-twined hands, then into Deanne's expectant face. "G-g-gone."

"Yes, gone. But you always wear it. Is it lost?" Agatha Booth shook her head vigorously. "Is it put away somewhere?"

"Lin. Lin-da." She squeezed Deanne's hands.

"Okay, I'll ask Auntie Linda. Do you want me to read to you?"

A slow shake of the head. "Talk me."

"Talk to you. Okay, you're such a great audience, I will. I got a promotion, to Manager of a new Welcome Society." Agatha gur-gled her approval. "But I turned it down." A disapproving grunt. "Yes, I know. But it's too much paperwork and admin stuff. I'd never get to do home visits or training again."

Agatha shook their combined hands like they were about to cast dice. "Go h-h-high. High," she instructed.

"Yeah, yeah. I know," said Deanne, squirming. "It's better money, but it's so different from what I'm used to, what I like," she quickly added. Agatha banged their hands on her lap and Deanne smiled. The old woman was sharp. "No flies on you, Grandmom. Yes, I am just too scared to take it."

"Go high," she confirmed before lying back on the settee and shutting her eyes.

"Oh, there you two are!" gushed Linda, bustling in with a duster. "I thought you'd taken her back to the commune with you."

"Co-op," reminded Deanne tiredly.

"That's what I said. Now, what were you two talking about? You looked very conspiratory." She moved the Hummel figurines—treacherously close to Agatha's left elbow—to another end table, then spoke directly into the good left ear. "Not spilling the family secrets, were you, Mother?"

Agatha's face puckered before she shook her head. Deanne couldn't place the look, but didn't like it. "And even if she was," she joked, "it would still be keeping it in the family, right?"

Linda glared, then smiled. "I meant, this little household family. I am, after all, the primary caregiver. No one else can seem to find the time to clean up after an incontinent old woman and hand-feed her peas. Not to mention the doctors appointments! She goes once a week for something or another, don't you, Mother?"

"T-t-t-telling, Dee," stammered Agatha, a beseeching look at Deanne.

"What, tell me what, Grandmom?"

"Come on, Mother, up you get; by the time we get you settled for the night, it'll be ten o'clock and I still have to make the icing for your cake. My Lord, what was I thinking, having forty-five people over?"

"Tell," repeated Agatha.

"She's saying she doesn't like me to tell her what to do," interpreted Linda, pulling at Agatha's elbow. "Left, left, Mother, we're going down the hall. What I wouldn't give to be able to beam you in and out of rooms like a Star Trek character."

Deanne filled the next morning completing the most inconspicuous jobs she could volunteer for, like raking the lawn and sweeping out the garage. Roger played bocce ball, as he did every Saturday without fail. Dave had some crisis with a shipment and spent the morning on his cell.

At only three o'clock, despite an invitation for four o'clock, guests started arriving. "Trust old folks to arrive early to the point of inconvenience," muttered Linda to Selma as they simultaneously scrambled out of their aprons and hid them under the sink.

Deanne stood helplessly in the kitchen, shoving trays and platters around the granite-topped island, trying to appear helpful. She flipped the smoked salmon off two teeny pumpernickel squares and was popping them into her mouth when Linda returned from the front door. "Deanne! Stop picking at them and get them into the living room!"

At least it was something constructive to do.

Her mother was already making the rounds of chatting seniors, a plate of sizzling pork medallions of some kind in one hand and festive serviettes in the other. Selma looked at Deanne, surveying again with a cheery smile. "Here, honey, why don't I take those?" she offered in a tight voice. "You obviously haven't had time to change." She spoke half to Deanne and half to the wizened couple on the couch, one with a sherry and one with tea. "But don't be long, honey, because we're going to have speeches soon." The tone had changed to a hiss.

Deanne chewed at the inside of her cheeks. She had changed, at least from the chore clothes of the morning.

In the guest bathroom, she examined herself in the mirror. Okay, so she wasn't Princess Diana—Goddess rest her soul, she automatically intoned. Two of the layers of her Indian tier-skirt had tiny sagging rips. Damn. She'd meant to fix them on the ferry. And the faint ketchup stain was still there, but only if you knew where to look, she reasoned. There was no way she could improve on the only shoes she'd brought—Doc Martens—no one else in the family wore size six. Her top was a long-sleeved, scooped-neck khaki tee. Thank Goddess she'd actually thought to put on a bra before leaving the apartment the previous morning. Deanne rummaged through Selma's portion of the guest room closet. One navy skirt wasn't *that* bad. But would they prefer her barefoot or in what they all termed "the clodhoppers"?

Deanne flopped down on the bed, staring at the intricately stippled ceiling. Grandmom was blind, for Heaven's sake; what was the big deal about dressing up?

In the end, she wore her mother's navy skirt with too-big gold-toed sandals that screamed "Palm Spring Old People's Resort" which she found in the back of the closet. They flapped against her heels, announcing her approach before she entered a room. Linda would like that. A skinny red lettuce elastic served to hold half of her hair off her face, cowgirl-style. In the further spirit of concession, Deanne applied two swipes of an abandoned tube of Palisades Pink lipstick, retrieved from the second drawer of the vanity.

Selma sighed heavily when Deanne presented herself back in the kitchen. Deanne scowled, though she knew it was immature. Why did she always feel twelve at these family gatherings instead of twenty-seven?

"At least I'm here, Mom," she snapped before moving into the living room. Linda, also in the kitchen to replenish her cucumber sandwich tray, didn't have time to comment, as both the side and front doorbells were chiming regularly.

Deanne was grateful that it wasn't her who spilled the punch. Linda could hardly be anything but gracious and forgiving to the minister of the First Baptist Church, whose fire-and-brimstone services she and Agatha attended every week.

"Oh, my goodness, and all over the birthday girl! I am so sorry, Linda," he gushed.

"Better the birthday girl than the carpet," Deanne heard Linda sizzle under her breath. Then, louder, "Not to worry, Reverend Gold; poor Mother is always spilling things on herself. I have another outfit already laid out on her bed, just in case. It will just take a jiffy for me to change her and then we'll do the cake. I'm counting on you for a quick, a *lovely*, grace."

Agatha sat patting her wet lap with her functional arm, looking forlorn. "Sorly. Sor-ry, Lin."

"Oh, for Heaven's sake, Mother; it wasn't your fault for once!" She cackled loudly and looked around at the anxious faces. "Perhaps she thinks she's wet herself!" The Reverend took the opportunity to scuttle away. After using all available serviettes—of superior quality and absorbency—Linda looked crossly around the room until she spied her husband, talking animatedly with the home care lady, whose spiked heels, Deanne noticed, made deep rivets in the plush carpet. "Roger? Roger! Come here. Go make fresh coffee; I've got to change Mother." He stared at her blankly for a moment, then resumed his conversation. To no one in particular, Linda seethed, "Obviously, as usual, I have to do everything around here."

Deanne stepped in. "Here, I'll help Grandmom. You make coffee."

"No," directed Linda, "you make coffee. I'm quicker at getting her in and out of her clothes."

"Linda," said Deanne, deliberately leaving out the familial title, "you don't want me making your coffee; trust me. I don't drink the stuff and wouldn't make it to your standards. Come on, Grandmom. Come with me."

Linda was determined not to relinquish her grip on Agatha's elbow. "Well, where's your mother? Your mother makes bearable coffee."

"Giving a tour to the McDougals," answered Deanne, putting her arm around Agatha and starting to propel her in the right direction.

"A tour? A tour of my house? She might go in the messy rooms; my God, she'll go and show Roger's atrocity of a den. What was she thinking?" With a last helpless look at Deanne, Linda scooted down the hallway, calling for her sister.

When she clicked the door closed, Deanne wished she could stay in her grandmother's bedroom for the rest of the afternoon. She felt ten years old again, with an acute yearning to sift through Agatha's magical jewelry box and its promises of bygone glamour and family history.

A yellow dress, very similar to the stained one, lay on the bed. Even with their big front buttons and elastic waists, it would be impossible for Agatha to manage the switch on her own. Deanne let her shuffle along the wall towards the bed. Agatha sat when she reached the high mattress and shunted her gaze methodically around the room.

"Look. Look." She crooked a finger toward the dresser. "G-g-one."

"Look where?" quizzed Deanne. "Where do I look?"

Agatha pulled at her fingers and the crepey skin around her neck. "Ju."

Desperately, Deanne tried to understand. "Oh! Jewelry? You want your jewelry box."

This was confirmed by Agatha's braying. Deanne took it from the dresser and placed it in the senior woman's lap. "Here, Grandmom. Your jewelry box." She guided Agatha's right, gnarled hand to balance the delicate receptacle while coaxing the left hand to open it.

Agatha clumsily patted the items within, prodded the box's special nooks and pockets. "Gonnnnnnnnnnnnnnnne," she wailed, pushing the mahogany box to the floor, where its colourful contents scattered like spilled Smarties.

At a loss, Deanne could only coo and cajole into the good ear. "Well, now they're all over the place. Your treasures. Stay still or you'll step on an earring. Why did you do that?"

"Bahad girl."

Deanne softened. "Not bad, Grandmom. You're impatient and a little on the crotchety side, no offence, but you're not bad." She didn't understand the deep growling sound that emanated from Agatha as she concentrated on pairing up each set.

"Here, now stand up. We're supposed to be changing your party dress. I'll do everything." Agatha stood, opening and closing her mouth, as powerless as a baby during a diaper change.

Deanne peeled off the soiled dress, letting it drop to Agatha's feet. She was prepared to view the creepy skin of the aged, the deep-purple spiderweb veins and liver spots shaped like countries, the sagging flesh.

She wasn't prepared for the bruises, the motley collection of circles in various shades of brown and yellow that spotted the matriarch's arms and legs. A particularly large contusion on her upper right thigh looked the newest. Deanne's gasp didn't escape the old woman, completely vulnerable and exposed in her brassiere and underwear. She began rocking back and forth under Deanne's stare, humming an indistinguishable tune.

Still, Deanne made light. "Grandmom! You're one big bruise! What've you been doing to yourself? Have you been practicing WWF wrestling again with the boy across the street?"

The humming stopped and they found each other's eyes.

Deanne's were wide and searching, Agatha's filmy and vacant. She used her good arm to point at her chest. "Me, no. No."

"No wrestling with boys?" Deanne repeated, shaking off Agatha's eerie gaze.

There was an anguished howl, a frustrated smack to Deanne's elbow. And again, Agatha was pointing. "Nobah. Juthold. Ol lade. Nobaaaad."

Deanne strained to understand. "You're not bad, I got that. Just hold you? You want me to hold you?" She outstretched her arms but Agatha shook her head.

"Juts old. No bad. See-cret."

Deanne processed the tingly, raw-skin feeling washing over her body. "You have a secret?" A decisive nod. "Can you tell me more?"

"Bad gu-erl."

"Who? You're a bad girl?" A ferocious shake of her head.

"Linna. Linna hur. Linna hurrrrrrrrrrrrt."

Deanne pressed her index fingers hard into her eyeballs, feeling the wetness seep out anyway. "Oh, Grandmom. Linda hurts you? Linda hits you?" she tried to confirm, her voice quavering like the senior's. Agatha responded by dropping her head, whether in prayer or shame, Deanne couldn't tell. The pose struck her as unbearably pathetic, and she was spurred to hustle the rigid figure into the clean dress. "Okay. It's okay. I'll help you. I'll figure it out."

Linda's appearance at the doorway didn't surprise Deanne, understanding now why her aunt wouldn't want them to be left alone. "What's taking you gals? The ice cream is melting and I want those codgers out by six." She glared at both of them.

Agatha rocked and hummed; Deanne stared back. "There's a problem, Deanne May?"

"You and I will be talking. Tonight. You have some explaining to do."

Linda flicked her eyes up and down Agatha, assessing before responding. "Don't be so dramatic, Deanne. You're always so dramatic. You're as bad as Mother. Return to my party, the both of you immediately. I don't have all day to listen to your theatrics."

Deanne spent the rest of the party sitting on the arm of the birthday girl's decorated party chair, a hand never leaving Agatha's shoulder. Selma was clearly annoyed that she wasn't in the kitchen helping.

At precisely six, Linda started banging dishes around until the stragglers took the hint and gave one last greeting and kiss to Agatha. Roger had been banished to his den for telling a slurred and questionably appropriate anecdote about Rancine, the local diner waitress. Dave sprawled and burped in the TV room. Deanne and her mother were in the kitchen alone, having settled Agatha in the living room with one of her new books-on-tape.

Linda entered full force, faltered, and looked as if she were about to back up.

"No, come in, Auntie Linda. I was just going to tell Mom."

"There's still some teacups in the . . ." she started.

"Never mind the damn teacups. Mom, I think—no, I know—Linda is abusing Grandmom."

"Oh, for Heaven's sake," retorted the sisters in perfect, scoffing unison.

"Tell her, Linda. Tell her! You know I saw the bruises."

"Selma, you know how often she falls and bumps into things. Old skin like that bruises from a hug. Three days ago, she missed the chair and ended up on her tush; a few days before that, she banged her shin on the toilet bowl after dropping her toothbrush."

"Grandmom told me, Linda. Told me."

"Pfffffffttt," exhaled Linda. "If you can figure out what Mother is muttering on about, you're a better person than I."

"Yes, well, that may be true," Deanne snarled. She faced Selma. "Mom, I saw the bruises; they're all over her body and she told me, 'Linda hurt.' Go talk to Grandmom if you don't believe me."

Thwack! went the dishcloth on the counter. "I will not put up with these ridiculous accusations in my own house. Little Miss Granola Girl, if you continue to slander me for taking care of my own mother, I will ask you to leave. Is that clear?"

"I'll be glad to. And I'll take Grandmom with me."

"You silly, silly child; you could no more take care of her than Dave, or Roger, or any one of you could." She refrained from naming Selma specifically, knowing the boundaries.

For her part, Selma watched them both, her eyes reflecting first annoyance, then wariness, then fear, and finally, outrage. "Linda, what the hell is she talking about?"

Linda shrugged. "Do I know? She's probably high on some drug. In fact, I think you should leave my house this instant. I don't house drug addicts."

"Yeah! Only elder-abusers! Mom, do something, Mom!" pleaded Deanne.

"Well, honey, your grandmother does take a lot of turns; I've witnessed a couple of doozies."

"Mom!" she cried again. "I am a lot of things you don't want me to be, like a vegan and an uncertified social worker and husband-less, but Mom, I've never outright lied to you about anything in my life. You have to listen to me!"

Selma's lips pressed tightly together.

The clattering of the cane made them look to the kitchen

doorway. Agatha had silently joined them and was leaning against the door frame, her bad arm dangling beside her like a wet rag on a hook. She pushed away from the frame and moved toward Linda.

"Bah-had daug. Daug. Daug-t-t-t-e-r." Her good hand pawed at the space in front of Linda's face. "Huuuuuuuuurt." She tottered to one of the kitchen drawers, hitting the counter above the cutlery drawer repeatedly. Deanne opened it and stood back. Agatha clawed through its contents, seemingly meaninglessly. When she clasped onto what she wanted, a large soup ladle, she made a baying sound and started hitting herself in the chest and stomach. "Stu-pid, Mah-ther. Bad." Deanne leapt across the kitchen and wrenched the utensil from her hand.

Selma threw both hands across her mouth, like a child about to throw up.

"I trusted you," she gasped through her hands. "I trusted you with my mother. What kind of animal would terrorize her own helpless mother?"

"You! You know nothing. You and your four-hundred dollars a month contribution, you know nothing! You know nothing of what it's like, day after day, wiping bottoms and spit-up. Being chained to this house when I should be on a cruise, lunching with girlfriends. All because she," Linda spat, "won't go to a home and you won't back me up."

Selma looked genuinely bewildered. "But we decided, we discussed that it was better that you take her, with the extra room and all. And Roger, you have Roger to . . ."

"Drunken ass!" shouted Linda toward the den. "That drunken ass is only another burden. Go to hell, all of you." Her colouring was dangerously gray. "Go fuck yourselves!"

Deanne reeled. No Biggs/Booth/Waterfell woman over forty had ever publicly uttered the F-word.

"Soap!"

They gawked at Agatha, who looked triumphant, her cheeks flushed as apple-red as a schoolgirl's. She made clucking sounds and repeated, "Soap your moouuuuth for c-c-c-c-ussing."

Part of Deanne wanted to laugh at the maternal threat. She shook her head to keep focused. "And what about the jewelry? She says you're stealing her jewelry. Like the ruby ring."

Linda stared at Deanne blankly, then melted into high-pitched laughter. "My God, you think I'm stealing jewelry too? Call the constabulary. Better yet, just shoot me now."

"Well, some's missing," said Deanne, her tone wavering, "and I don't even know half of what to look for."

With bravado, Linda yanked open the cupboard next to the microwave and pulled out an unlidded, old-fashioned flour canister. She spilled the tin's glittering gold, silver, and gemstone contents onto the island. "There! There, you sanctimonious little brat. She," Linda explained, now with eerie calm, jerking her head at Agatha, "has been stashing different bits in here for months. At first, I kept putting them back; I tried to explain that her gifts or safekeeping weren't necessary, but she's such a busy beaver, I finally gave up."

Deanne felt the teeniest drop of urine escape her body, and her left eye vibrated convulsively. "I'm sorry. I'm so, so sorry. About that part."

"You're abusing our mother?" Selma whispered.

The question crumpled Linda and she began sobbing. "Once, twice. A smack. Nothing more. You don't understand." The rest of her explanation became as incomprehensible as most of Agatha's.

"Come on, little sister," coached Selma, her voice shaky. "Let's get you to bed. Do you have any tranquilizers? Brandy?" Together, they swayed down the hall. Deanne winced. Two Agathas in the making.

Agatha and Deanne gazed around the kitchen for several minutes and let the electricity in the air recede. Then Deanne gathered the frail woman in her arms.

"All b–b–b–better?" Agatha stuttered.

Deanne leaned a little to the right, to better reach the good ear. "Yes, all better. Everything will be okay now. We'll help Auntie Lin. I love you, Grandmom."

"Love too," came the muffled response as they stood together and rocked.

Finally, Agatha pushed away and lifted her eyes to Deanne's. She winked awkwardly, then most articulately chirped, "All better. Ice cream now, Dee-Dee."

On Laurel's Nightstand

This is what's on Laurel's nightstand: tweezers, two glue-on nails that resemble shiny but misshapen red Smarties, a fat plastic syringe used for inserting contraceptive foam, toast crumbs, a blob of cinnamon butter, and a tall, narrow glass with fake-gold curly-cues faded by the dishwasher. If the glass's remaining contents were analyzed, they would be deemed 90 per cent Vancouver tap water and 10 per cent Glacier Berry cider. What's on her nightstand is revealing, but not nearly as revealing as what's on Laurel herself.

On Laurel, there are thirty-one years, a bra slung over one shoulder like a backpack, toast crumbs and several smears of cinnamon butter, a crusting glob of contraceptive foam and semen in her pubes, and the million-pound arm of Dan the twenty-year-old Cactus Club waiter. Ooops, *Server*. She prefers to proceed mutually nameless, but he'd had that damn nametag.

It is presently dark. Darkish. Her sublet, tenth-floor loft at the corner of Seymour and Nelson does not get dark. Or quiet. Ever. It is 2:37 on a Tuesday morning and she is still hearing breakups and breakdowns; they drift up from the spillage of the adjacent bars.

Fuck you, Judd! I'm noise noise noise *yeah you too!*

noise noise noise *I love you, Terry.*

Car alarm.

I'm gonna puke noise noise noise *pepperoni* noise.

Cop, ambulance, or fire-truck siren. Or just a dickhead howling.

Therefore, Laurel loves rain because it motivates the nightcrawlers to scurry into cabs and buses a shitload faster and quieter.

She lies, eyes wide open, gazing over the solid hills and valleys that form her body, comforted by the insulation they provide. Her eyes narrow, catlike, when she thinks about the old Laurel. Bone rack. Feeble. *No goddamn wonder . . .*

She knows it's time when her skin begins to itch where his hands have fumbled. Into the quasi-darkness, when she can stand it no more, Laurel says, "You have to leave." There is no response, so she pushes off his cedar tree of an arm and repeats, "Hey! I want you to leave now!"

It's only when she gets up and thwacks on the overhead light that the Cactus Club Server finally awakes.

"Frig, man."

He is suddenly not cute. Not cute enough to sleep with, to bring home, and maybe not even cute enough for the 20 per cent tip he received six hours previous.

He is, however, young and consequently erect. Again. Laurel sees this through the thin Indian cotton bedsheet—all anyone can stand in the loft, whose August air is as thick and warm and sickeningly sweet as inhaling the air created by microwaved waffles. "Hey, don't kick me out now, baby, I'm . . ." he begins.

She ignores his penis and his plea. "Out. You're a guy; it's no big deal. You can take safe night walks and buses and strolls on the beach and no one will bug you."

"I live in West Van," he whines. "There's no buses now."

Laurel didn't know this. Hadn't bothered to ask.

But then, had He asked? Had He asked anything about her before pushing her down onto the rocks of Jericho Beach? No, He had not.

"Get out!" she shouts, quite frantically, alarming them both. His Gap model face expresses a combination of lust, bewilderment, and plain ripped-offness. "Get out!" A shrill scream.

He pulls on his Roots T-shirt and black cargo pants, balls his who-cares-what-coloured gaunch into one of the pockets, shoves bare feet into his trendy Mountain Equipment Co-op sandals, and stomps downstairs and out the door. Preppie geek. Wanted to fuck an aging punker. A new-waver. Whatever he thought the spiky blonde and green hair and the studs made her.

Alone, Laurel yowls *fuuuuccccckkkkk* and wonders if they can hear her on the street as easily as she hears them.

Nobody heard that night.

The alarm goes off in the morning; Laurel tosses back the watery cider to open her throat and calls in sick to the sugar factory on McGill.

It is the seventh time this month. She has been labelled by her boss and colleagues as lazy, ungrateful, a druggie, a faker, on one hell of a long rag, and a shopaholic. The last one makes Laurel laugh; they only ever see her in stained uniforms and hairnets. How do they know if she has a buying fetish? How the hell do they know anything about her at all? It is the twenty-seventh of

August and she vows to show up—starting tomorrow—for the rest of the month.

The next time Laurel looks at the clock it is 1:33 PM. She rolls over and clicks on *Coronation Street, Rosie, Oprah,* and follows up with *That 70s Show.* Then, in a burst of productivity, she Comets the bathroom and is rewarded by finding an errant earring in the cleaning supply cabinet. She scrounges enough quarters and loonies for two loads of laundry, even adjusting the dials to reflect big/small, hot/cold, which she rarely bothers with.

It's all big. It's all very cold.

At 6:14, her girlfriend Jada, who is twenty-nine and has three kids and umpteen boyfriends, calls and asks Laurel if she wants to hit Taco Time and cheap night at the movies. Cheap night. Even cheap night eats ten, eleven bucks. Laurel says no, she'll stay home and make a plan.

"Ohhhh," says Jada sarcastically. "It's *Plan* Night."

"Fuck off, and what's that supposed to mean?" retorts Laurel.

"Fuck off? Means to screw one's . . ."

"You know what I mean." Laurel also knows what Jada means, but decides to torture them both anyway.

But Jada won't play. "Never mind. Call me when you're done getting it together and if you're not too good for me, we'll go out."

Laurel props herself up in bed, which reeks of Cactus Club french-fry grease and young-buck sweat. Should have done three loads of laundry. She holds a child's scribbler with a few pages of math problems—obviously abandoned in her apartment by one of Jada's monkeys—a Bic pen, and the rest of the cider.

The Plan is:

quit sugar factory. get job as receptionist at car dealership

quit fast sex. get rich boyfriend over thirty-five.
quit junk food. eat healthy. veg, fish, etc.
quit drinking
quit picking at self

Laurel guzzles and thinks.

quit with the tight clothes. dress classy. kill the green hair.
forget about all the shit-past and move on

She doodles a daisy after this last idea, then colours in all the numbers with round bits on the previous pages. She reads over the list again and is aware of something like a serrated fingernail scratching incessantly at her brain. She shakes her head to dislodge it.

"Stop it," she commands aloud. "Stop, stop, stop, stop it!"

Laurel tosses the pen and scribbler in the direction of the nightstand and picks up the tweezers. In what might be seen by outsiders as a tawdry erotic display, she tilts the gooseneck lamp this way and that, until it shines satisfactorily onto the Brillo pad muff between her legs. The heat from the bulb is soothing.

Frantically at first, starting from the left, she yanks the stray pubic hairs that creep out of the perfect triangle. After the cursory go, she gouges deeper, the needle-nose tips seeking any bit of growth, like shell-seekers on a pillaged coast. Little red bumps, hard and pulsing, appear as quickly as she plucks and bring satisfaction. A release, anyway.

Only when she begins cramping from the convoluted position, and the tender skin has been ravaged, does Laurel toss the tweezers back onto the rubble of the nightstand and yank off the lamp. She takes in the last of the cider and attempts to place the empty plastic bottle on the nightstand, but it falls over, rolls off, and hits the floor with a series of hollow-sounding *clunks*. Very hollow sounding. She lies in the dark. Extra dark tonight.

The Last Dinner Pary

I am standing in front of the fridge, the freezer part, surveying the various mysterious and double-wrapped packages in search of dinner, when he dumps the news on me.

"Oh, I forgot to tell you, Anala phoned and invited us over for dinner."

The cold mist swirling out of the compartment is not enough to cool my face as it flushes instantly at this announcement. I thrust my head in deeper and suck in the air.

"Okay? Did you hear me?" asks my husband, Ted, wandering by and swatting my butt.

I pull out perogies and what feels to be chicken wings, through the plastic, anyway, and toss them into the sink. *Thunk thunk*. "I'm not really up to it," I say, putting my head back in, wishing for a bag of frozen corn or peas to mold around my face.

"You can have a nap; we don't have to leave for over an hour." He massages my neck and shoulders, as he has taken to doing lately.

I wriggle away. "It's not the tired thing. I just feel like staying in."

"Jess," he says, irritation gestating in his voice, "we've stayed in a lot lately. Tons. It would really mean a lot to me if we could get out." He managed to pull his tone together. "Please? And hey, if it's about . . ."

"Stop," I warn, punctuating the demand by slamming the freezer door.

I stand fingering the icy packages, silent until he pulls them out of the sink and returns them to the freezer. I wonder if my colouring has receded to its usual mozzarella-white. "What did she say? Exactly."

"She said, 'Do you guys want to come over for dinner? It's been a while.'"

"Do you think it was her idea?"

He gives me his *Is this an estrogen thing?* look—an expression that started just after the spontaneous backrubs—and scratches his head of blond, cherub curls.

"It's important to me," I snap, not caring that I have sworn off snapping and all its derivatives. "Do you think Raj wants us to come too?"

He groans, like a dog that knows it must endure the bumpy car ride before getting to the beach. "I'd assume so! She said he's working until six. Why would you even ask that?"

I look down my shirt, past the spaghetti sauce stain from lunch, past the straining zipper of my jeans, all the way down to my sock-covered feet. They also sport a crusting plop of spaghetti sauce. "Never mind," I mumble.

I go upstairs and curl up on top of the bed, ostensibly to doze, but I end up in an alternate cycle of wallow and churn.

Shit. Shit. Double-shit.

We stop at a Chinese grocery to buy tulips for Anala, and get a six-pack at the off-license for Ted. I wait in the car, obsessing about the billowy peasant dress I chose to wear, picking at my face in the teeny sunscreen mirror, puckering and unpuckering my lips of painted Coral Explosion.

"You look great," Ted assures, getting back in the car and handing me the beer and flowers. I continue fussing with my home-cut dirty-blonde bangs.

"I hate this. I hate, hate, hate this. I always have, and you know it," I add before he can ask why, which he does anyway. "Because, Anala is too perfect. Too pretty, too pert. I'm totally intimidated by her."

"You're nuts. She likes you; otherwise, why would she invite us for dinner?"

"She likes *you*," I say crossly, the back of my eyeballs starting to hurt from the ridiculous hypocrisy of this whole thing.

He knows how I mean it, but snorts anyway and pats my leg. Ted is one of those ruddy, but cuddly, bear-types. Safety is always found within his arms. Suddenly, he is pulling into their driveway and it's much too soon. I need them to live farther away.

Anala and Raj, as a couple, have been our casual friends for two years now. It started when I was hired as a consultant for the art design of Raj's monthly magazine devoted to the Indo-Canadian community. Since then, we'd done the dinner-and-a-movie thing a couple of times, cocktails, stuff like that. Anala makes fabulous Indian food and Raj has a four hundred-plus CD collection.

Everybody kisses and hugs at the door and we get all that "it's been far too long" crap out of the way. Even these few and far-between rendezvous were supposed to have ceased, according to my secret and sole dictum. I hug Raj, as angular and sculpted as ever, but avoid meeting his gaze, and watch over his shoulder at Anala patting Ted's stomach.

"Little winter hibernation issues here, Ted? I hate to tell you, but it's almost April."

He grossly distends his stomach in lieu of his tongue and says, "I'm eating for two."

"It smells great," I interrupt, and motion to the stovetop of pots, vibrating with heat. "Of course, it always does," I add. *Unlike the time you came to my place and the bubbled-over grease from the meat-loaf set off the smoke detector and drove us all onto the roof with pizza.*

"Okay," says Raj, ushering us into the living room. He rubs his hands together like a mad scientist and asks, "What's your poison, guys?"

Ted says beer, like always. I say water, like never. "It's a calorie thing," I explain to abate Raj's disbelief. "You know, the post-Christmas pledge to cut back."

It occurs to me how sad it is that I'd rather him think me an alcoholic than anything else.

He shakes his head, indicating he thinks us lost causes. "You two are both stuck in hibernation."

Of course, I still have not looked directly at him, even when I know he's just looking at me in his host-with-the-most way. Or otherwise.

So we sit around their cozy living room, which is full of taste-ful, ethnic art that whispers money and connections to more than a touristy Bombay street artist. Anala sits on the arm of the couch so she can pop up and down to stir the contents of those bubbling pots. When Raj is gone to get Ted another beer and himself another G&T, Ted hisses at me, "What is wrong with you?"

"Nothing," I hiss back, though I am tempted to just ignore him.

"You're barely saying anything and you've spent the last half-hour staring at the walls."

"I'm looking at the artwork and by the way, thank you for the warm expression of concern."

He rolls his eyes but manages to eke out, "Jessie, please? Tell me why you're so tense."

"Just don't forget the deal," I smile sweetly as our hosts re-enter the room arm-in-arm. I give Raj some glazed eye contact. They cloud. His big brown eyes cloud and quiver.

"We can eat," announces Anala, moving back into the kitchen. Ted jumps up and is standing near the dining room table before I've even uncrossed my legs. Or my fingers. Raj and I are left alone in the living room.

"Hi," he mouths.

I nod my acknowledgement.

"You okay?"

I take a step toward him and murmur, "I'm sorry about this; I wasn't told early enough to get out of it."

He grimaces in commiseration. "Me neither. Maybe it's destiny."

I scoot around him at that, head down and arms tight against my sides, like a nun passing a naked statue that is not papal-blessed.

But I'm no nun.

"Who's for wine?" queries Raj when we're all seated before a buffet of Indian delectables that's enough to feed a village. Usually, I am the Queen of Curries, but a searing pillar of heartburn rises just looking at the steaming bowls of pungent yellows, reds, and oranges.

"Jess, wine?"

I shake my head.

"You're sure? You don't have to teetotal on our account," he cajoles, doing this hula dance thing with the bottle.

"Raj! Stop it. She doesn't have to drink." Anala tousles her childhood sweetheart's hair before reaching for the *chapatis*. "But you do all have to eat," she adds triumphantly. "*Dal*, Ted? Raj, pass Jess the *bhajias*; they're her favourite."

We eat and chat. I serve myself my usual amount, but mostly stir it around the plate and come to admit that it's not about the food's spice. I sit with my knees clamped chastely together, so when I feel the nudge of Raj's foot to my left, I know it's no accident.

There once was a dinner, at this very same table, when I surreptitiously peeled off his sport-sock with my toes and balled it beneath my chair for the secret laugh of watching him squirm.

After dinner, Raj brings out photo albums—an act I perceive as utterly cruel and for which I could kill him—and we all squish onto the couch to review their lives. The propane fireplace is cranked on high. Raj, Anala, and Ted are sipping some kind of cognac, but I am the one spiralling into a simulated drunk, where deep breaths and constant movement are required to maintain composure. The images come and go like those in a Viewfinder toy.

Anala and Raj in their high-school graduation gowns.

Raj in a pale-blue leisure suit at somebody's wedding.

Anala sunning on a Caribbean beach, '94 scratched in the sand beside her.

An off-centre Raj and Anala cuddling on the couch we sit on now, the couch I swear has been sent to sea.

"That was done with the self-timer," inputs Anala, apparently eager to explain the photo's less-than-perfect composition.

"Let's go back to your bikini pics," pipes up Ted. Anala giggles, and Raj flips the plasticized pages back, grunting and pointing like an aroused caveman when he finds them again.

"My woman, ug, ug, ug."

The flames are filling the whole cavity of the fireplace. The three of them bloat into my space; their hot, curried, and liquored breaths swirl around me. The couch is rocking.

"Ted, we should go," I say. It seems loud, but no one acknowledges me; they are hysterical over an eight-by-ten of Raj with permed hair from 1979.

The lentils and chicken and basmati rice in my belly are hysterical, too.

"Oh, that's my sister, pregnant with her first!" squeals Anala, as her champagne-coloured nail taps the one-dimensional, telltale bump of a woman stretched out on a La-Z-Boy. "Now she has five!"

"Five!" exclaims Ted, feeding into the photo/baby frenzy. "Holy cow!"

"Hey, watch the cow jokes, buddy; you're in sacred-cow country," responds Raj, trying to look stern.

Ted laughs and says, "Okay, then: holy *shit*. Besides, you're as Hindu as I am Catholic."

Raj spiels out some Hindi that is no doubt rude, but cracks up after ten seconds.

"I just can't imagine," continues Anala, seemingly oblivious to their buffoonery. "Five! I can't imagine having even one. What a responsibility."

"What a disruption," adds Raj, refocusing on his glowing

sister-in-law. "No more spontaneous trips to Nassau."

"But you'd still buy me diamonds and cars, right?" jokes Anala.

"Please, baby, my Harley is next."

I strain to get up, to push away the arms and legs entwined in mine. "Let me up," I gasp, then shriek, "I said, let me up. I'm going to be sick!"

They get it, finally, and part like the Red Sea, allowing me to surge into the bathroom.

I slam the door behind me, whirling around and bending over the pristine bowl just in time to direct the streams of gold and brown that gush from my gut.

Ted won't come inside or even to the door; he never does. Even the mere idea of puke freaks him out. Anala taps lightly when I am hanging off the empty towel rack, panting and waiting for another wave of purging.

I will never be empty enough; this I know.

"Jess? I'm putting a clean washcloth and towel outside the door, for after. Do you need anything else?" Her voice is concerned and motherly and utterly forgiving, though I have produced one of the more spectacular dinner-party shows.

"I'm okay," I croak, tears springing to my eyes as self-pity and shame replace urgency and desperation. I sense her move away from the door.

When I open it, just six inches, to pat around for the towels, a hand takes mine. Raj gently shoulders his way in, the towels from his wife under his arm. I don't have the strength to object. He runs the cold water full-force and clicks on the fan as sound decoys.

"Are you all right? Jesus Christ, I'm worried to death."

I take a wad of tissue, blow my nose, and finally look him right in the eyes. "Hey, it's not a matter of death; it's a matter of life." I bend into the sink to mix the icy water with my tears and can hear his hard exhale over the streaming water.

"Oh my God."

"Yeah? Which one?" Now I bury my face in the plush towel. It's so velvety and inexplicably warm, I wish my whole body were wrapped in it.

But Raj pulls the towel away and grabs my chin, directs it like a rudder and forces me to look at him again. "Is it mine?"

"No," I whisper, turning the water back on to garble our words. "It's been too long. I'm fourteen weeks."

"You said goodbye fourteen and a half weeks ago."

I am not surprised he has kept track; he could always recite even insignificant dates of our affair as easily as a standard prayer. Besides, this man loved me, and I him. Loved, love. I cannot begin to place a tense on it. "It's not yours. Ours. I'm absolutely positive. Don't worry."

He looks me up and down. "That explains your sudden insistence on condoms."

I shrug, but am not in a position to make it cocky. "Bingo. I hadn't forgotten my prescription when I went to the art conference in November; I'd deliberately gone off them."

"Fuck, Jess, is this what you want? I can't believe this is what you want."

I cannot lie to this man. I have never been able to lie to him about anything. I tried faking my way through our first meeting for his magazine, when I wasn't prepped, and he called my bluff instantly. "It's what he wants. Ted," I add, as if there might be another. "I owe him. He's been there for me. You know, when my mom was dying."

"I would have been there for you," Raj spits, suddenly angry.

"I would have been there for you. I *was* there for you, dammit, for two years."

"It's not the same. We were fabulous, the best, but . . . shit, you know all of this. I couldn't hurt Ted like that and I couldn't stand that Anala would be hurt either. All of my choices in life are based on what will make me feel the least guilty." I shiver. "Except falling in love with you, but that wasn't really a choice anyway."

My ex-lover thumps back against the door, pokes himself in the kidneys with the knob, and curses. "You could, however, stand to come to my house and torture me," he throws in petulantly.

"You know I had no control over that. But don't worry; it won't happen again, 'cause I'll figure something out to keep the four of us apart."

"Hey, Nurse Raj! Are you helping the patient recover, or killing her?" This is Anala, banging authoritatively on the door. It's a polite way of saying it's not appropriate for him to be in here with me.

"We're coming," he forces out with relative cheer.

Five minutes later, Ted and I leave as we arrived: with hugs and kisses, averted gazes, and one—no two—secretly battered souls. I consider whispering how sorry I am into his ear, but it seems to be just something to say, just something to assuage my guilt.

In the car, I recline the seat and feign sleep, but Ted talks anyway. Truly? Part of me doesn't even care that he might not be fit to drive.

"Man, I wanted to tell them you were pregnant so bad! Almost did a couple of times. You have to let us tell people now; it's been the three months you wanted to wait. Okay? Okay, can we?" *Huh, Ma? Can we, can we, can we?*

"Yeah, whatever," I say, and he hoots *Riiiiiight On!* and cranks up the radio.

When my son is born in September, he is red and bloody and wrinkled and perfect.

By the next day, his colouring has subdued to a tawny brown.

There will be another get-together with Raj and Anala, though I doubt Anala will play the gracious hostess this time.

Getting to Guelph

They have passed eighteen pull-off Irving Service Stations, nine Tim Horton coffee shops, five reminders on big green boards with white writing that they're headed west, and various similar signs touting the kilometres to various places to which Bethie has never been, but hopes to some-day go.

Breathe. Right now, all that matters is getting to Guelph.

Ed hadn't noticed Bethie tilt the passenger-side mirror to such a rakish angle that he—and more importantly, she—can only see the blur of the blue-black asphalt whizzing beneath. She did it when he was in the third Irving Big Stop they passed near Amherst, when he was out to buy roast-chicken potato chips and cherry cola: apparently the only store anywhere that sold both of those products. Ed made this run all the time, usually in his Safeway produce truck and not his Chevette, so Ed should know.

Bethie moves just her eyes as far left as they will go, until they hurt and quiver, trying to look at Ed, her ticket to Guelph, without being caught. Feigning indifference, indifference this side of disdain, is so very important to her. It had been real; it had been him, no matter what she'd said back then.

And he was here now, sure as that was the sixth Golden Arches sign coming up on the right.

If she'd tried to explain to her mother, Dollie McDonnell, her mother would've said, "Aach, that's something you picked up in all them books. And even so, you can't be all that messy in the head; you got that big fat scholarship, didn't yous? Yous got the big fat scholarship to the school that'll take you away from your old mum."

Her father? He'd probably crack her upside her unmessy head for such blasphemy about his best friend—or whatever the sin was called when it was a mere mortal. Something worse than mere slander. To be sure, Jack McDonnell would say, "Yous already got all the attentions with this goddamn scholarship; will you shad up and get these Jesus suitcases out the way?"

That was it, pretty much.

There are several hours of daylight driving left, if Ed is up to it (which she supposes he is, given that he's a long-haul truck driver and all). Even so, Bethie is starting to feel tighter and tighter, like a waistband during Christmas dinner, only the pushing is coming from the outside in. She begins to rub the palm of her right hand over a jagged bit of the door handle, and is just about to feel the familiar sweet, rhythmic, and bloody release, when Ed interrupts by slamming on the brakes to avoid hitting a skunk.

Finally, in northern New Brunswick—Bethie isn't sure where, having stopped reading green signs and counting McDonald's and

Timmy's hours before—Ed pulls into a cheesy, one-storey motel. She starts to get out, to go talk to the emaciated woman standing outside the glass door marked *Regis rati n* in disintegrating letters, but Ed tells her to stay put. There is something odd about the way the woman's shirt falls.

Oh, yeah, missing tit. Surgeons get any thrill when they cut like that?

"Your father gave me your share of the accommodation monies; don't you worry."

"I just want to see . . ." she falters.

"Two rooms? Is that wha'cher worried about?"

She shrugs, like she doesn't care, but yes, that's it.

Ed snorts and she has no idea what the snort means. Barely knew what his strained grunt meant, so many years ago.

Back around the provincial border, he'd said, "Do yous remember me from when you was a little shit?"

She'd shrugged then too; he'd snorted then too.

She watches him go in and swears he's wearing the same navy blue polyester pants as five years ago.

When Ed comes out, the one-breasted stick-woman comes out too, back to the stoop to smoke. "Got the next best thing," he announces. "Two beds. They're full up. We'll go for a nice supper with the money I saved your father."

Bethie looks around the parking lot. There are only three cars in front of the numbered, royal-blue doors.

Ed says, "Leave them luggages for later," and she's only too relieved, because she has to pee so badly. Her brother's old hockey bag with the broken zipper and the mustard-coloured hard-side valise, donated by the neighbours to the east, they hold her whole life. The unmessy head on her shoulders, the two suitcases in the back of Ed's Chevette: they'd be the sum total of seventeen years.

She moves to use the bathroom as soon as they walk in the room. It's clunky and dank with no window, and just as she is shutting the door, Ed's big hand reaches around and twists and twists the inside knob with the locking button until it only dangles, a partially severed limb. Then he gently and chastely shuts the door from the outside.

Now she knows for sure.

Bethie stands perfectly still in the bathroom, on dingy beige linoleum, and thinks of the day last week when her father came home and said Eddy McGuire was driving up to Ontario over the Labour Day weekend to pick up a rig and was driving Bethie to the University of Guelph. For free.

She could have said something then, but her mother would have only kept doing dishes and her father would have spluttered, "Jesus Christopher, girl, you got turned right uppity since that goddamn scholarship. I don't want to hear another word about such foolishness; Ed McGuire's a good man. It's done business and if you think there's money to fly you there, you may as well be consid'rin' a flight to the moon. Don't be so foolish about taking the damn ride; you're a grown-up now!"

Was a very roundabout acknowledgement. Ac now ed   me .

So Bookie Bethie—town bookworm, town freak—shut herself in her bedroom with the fat, manila-coloured envelope from the University and pored over its contents for the millionth time. She concentrated on the pictures of the normal-looking kids lounging on cement steps, dressed in lab coats and doing experiments, striding proudly across a stage in cap and gown, waving their diplomas like tickets to Timbuktu. Bethie doesn't care about the diploma: getting to Guelph is the final exam.

She keeps her back to the mirror as she undoes her jeans.

Levi's. Lives. Viles. Evils.

The pee goes on forever. She looks down at the long, baby-pink scar across her lower belly, where no one would notice, then caresses all the similar secret gashes and puncture marks here and there over her body, her self-inflicted map of life.

"Put'cher hair in them pigtails again," he instructs from outside. "And don't worry; I got the big snip-snip since that last time. No chance of my fellows getting up there this time."

In the dank bathroom, she looks around for something suitable to use, but since it is a cheap roadside motel, what isn't brought in daily by laconic housekeepers, is bolted down. There is nothing. In light of this, Bethie jumps up on the counter when she has finally finished peeing, balances on the two inches between the sink and the edge. Her feet meet sole to sole in the sink and she looks herself in the eye for the first time in five years. It's a pretty face, she decides, unmarred and unrevealing of what lies beneath.

"Hurry up," he calls from the other side, so close she thinks she feels his breath penetrate the clapboard door. "Come pay for yer ride to Guelph and then I'll take yous out for a nice steak dinner at the pub. Let's see if yous are any better than you was."

Bethie decides there will be no more secret scars. She apologizes to Jimmy McTavish for blaming him for her expanded twelve-year-old tummy. She says a final goodbye to the squawking thing Doc McPhee pulled from her guts and then whooshed off to unknown parts. She leans forward and begins bashing her forehead into the reflecting glass until blood begins filling her eyes and the pretty, unmarred face is no more, until she can no longer see anything but red.

Just get to guel h; ust get to gu lph; ust ge to g el h.

Coloured Things

Claire's drinking isn't bad enough to do anything about. Just ask her; she'll tell you. It's true, she doesn't stagger through the streets in shredded mittens and matted hair, tilting back abandoned beer cans hopefully, holding them over her mouth like eyedroppers. Nor does she wander aimlessly through the apartment in a flowing peignoir set, clutching an oily martini chock full of olives that look back at her with their evil red pupils. No, Claire gets up and goes to work on time, very rarely foggy from drink, and keeps everything from her finances to her finger-nails in good order.

She drinks normally. Perhaps a tiny bit more than what would be considered prudent by, say, her mother's standards. But apparently her mother is too conservative anyway. This is why she believes it's not bad enough to do anything about.

On this particular evening, she is at a friend's house with

others. Her vodka-soda glass is empty, and Claire offers to refill wineglasses, highballs, and beers while she is up topping up her own.

"Thanks, Claire," murmurs Maggie, who is explaining the contents of a photo album to Les, a man Claire just met. Les drinks Diet Coke with six lemon slices. At the beginning of the evening, he'd stated, quite firmly, "No, I don't drink," when pressed for his favourite poison. Not "I can't drink right now," implying he is on antibiotics, or "No, I'm not drinking tonight," implying it a singular choice. He must be one of those problem drinkers, Claire had decided, the ones that get all slobbery, or violent, or miss their children's dance recitals. Thank God she is fun and still responsible when she gets tipsy.

Alone in Maggie's kitchen, Claire replenishes her own glass first so she will have something to sip while exacting the arduous task of pouring the assigned two wines and one lite beer. Maggie is very well-to-do—a VP in a huge software firm—and has furnished the kitchen island with a liquor store's selection. Surrounded by casual-looking, but specifically placed, flickering candles, the umpteen bottles stand in a semicircle and are reflected in the overhead mirror. Claire shifts around the jewel-toned bottles, interspersing them with the somber browns until she is satisfied with the buzzing cocktail-party arrangement she has created. The ruby red grenadine stands beside the chocolate-coloured rye bottle; the blue Curaco, she moves to the far edge, until it nuzzles the emerald glass of the red-wine bottle. The crème de menthe is paired with a sparkling blush, and the like. She slides them around like Stars on Ice figurines.

Claire takes three gulps from her glass—she prefers them neat—then tops it up again by pouring first vodka, then soda, and then another generous dollop of vodka. This is how she pours her drinks, in layers. Maggie comes in with another empty glass and Claire pushes the vodka bottle to the side. The topping-up ritual is always done privately.

Not that there's anything weird about it. She just doesn't want to look like a liquor hog.

Back in the living room, Brian, Claire's quasi-new boyfriend, is talking to Geoff about the virtues, or not, of Canadian football. Ash, Karen, Karen's latest man, and Maggie's girlfriend are playing Scattergories and laughing uproariously around the coffee table. The other two couples on the couch sit and look fairly bored.

How rude they look. Claire rearranges her face so it no longer twins theirs.

Nobody is rip-roaring drunk, and nobody will become so, including Claire. It's not that kind of party and Claire, of course, is not that kind of drinker. Despite Maggie's display of intoxicants, her parties never become rambunctious, because she invites the kind of people who are very likely to become clients of one another at some point. The lawyers remember the real estate agent they met at a Maggie-party when they want to move; the real estate agents might ask investment advice from the brokers, and so on. Maggie manages their companies' IT systems. Claire is an interior designer, which is how she'd met Maggie, and is in present and desperate need of new clients. Anyway, none are about to toss down their professionalism for the sake of one more imported beer.

Claire expects they save that for behind closed doors.

She stops drinking at eleven, for she had promised Brian she would drive home and is, essentially, sober by one o'clock when they say their goodbyes. She whooshes off to find her purse and coat and sees that her merry cocktailers have been marched back into their precise arc. Maggie is just like that, orderly and straight-up. An enviable quality.

Which Claire could have if she wanted, of course.

When Brian drops by her apartment at exactly happy hour, but without notice, a few days later, Claire tells him she acciden-tally dropped the remains of the vermouth, and cajoles him into a spicy Caesar instead of his usual vodka martini. She carefully makes the story both funny and tragic. This quick thinking is necessary because he'd left a new bottle last time he was over—was it only three days ago?—and now it is almost gone.

Brian is smooth and rumpled at the same time, a combination of prep and jock, and Claire loves this. She craves each side's approval. She settles him in the living room with a stack of the lat-est design magazines and bustles into the kitchen.

There is one inch of vodka left. Claire holds the bottle under the tap and fills it to an arbitrary five-inch mark, then completes the drink. She pours more wine for herself into one of her deceased grandmother's sparkling Waterfords and plops the gas-station tum-bler from which she has been drinking into the dishwasher.

Brian follows her into the kitchen when she goes to pour seconds.

"Hey! Did you have a party I missed out on?" he exclaims when he sees the three inches left in the vodka bottle: the three inches of chlorinated city water.

Claire's heart goes *thud thud thump.* "Oh, God no! Well, a girl, a window-dresser from work—Lynn?—anyway, she came over because she broke up with her boyfriend. It was a bit of a wicked Monday night, that's for sure. I meant to replace it for you; I just haven't had a chance."

"No sweat," says Brian amiably. He is that kind of guy: couldn't lie if his life depended on it, but is easily lied to. Claire both adores and despises this quality. "As long as you're not harbouring another man who's drinking my Smirnoff. Doing the deed with you, yes; drinking my Smirn, no way."

"Ha, ha," she chirps happily and hands him the Caesar, heartily laced with Worcestershire, lemon juice, and Tabasco. "There are no other men of whom I am aware anyway."

Get the fuck outta my kitchen.

"Hey! I just remembered," Brian exclaims. "You know Geoff, from the party? OD'd on crack two days ago. Died. Died!"

"Yikes. Really? I'd only met him a few times. He didn't seem like he had a drug problem, did he?"

"No," Brian agrees, the slightest of quizzical looks passing over his face after his first sip. "But I've always believed addictions are harder to spot in people with money. You know, the ones that sleep in a good bed, who have access to a long, hot shower the morning after a tear, women who have makeup tricks up their sleeves. The poor ones who wake up on a park bench, well, what cover do they have?"

"If it was me, I'd just die of embarrassment," Claire says. The irony eludes her.

"Got any nibblies? Pretzels, maybe?"

"Sorry, no." The salty, cardboard swirls had been uncontrollably consumed along with two cups of mayonnaise. They were tasty at the time, but left Claire violently retching at two AM. Vodka and mayo and pretzels obviously didn't agree. Somewhere, she'd read that the loopy pretzel shape represented praying hands. "But let's order a pizza. My treat."

There are many ways to purge the guilt of drinking a man's vodka.

Like later, when Claire pushes herself much further sexually than she is comfortable, even surprising Brian, until she feels penance has been sufficiently paid. Only then does she allow herself to fall asleep in his arms.

After another few weeks, apparently Brian thinks Claire is normal (had she not said so herself?) and worthy enough to meet his parents, and he proposes they drive the three hours north so she can be officially introduced. She agrees whole-heartedly, feels flattered. Brian accepts her for who she is, totally. She vows to fake nothing in his presence.

The next Saturday afternoon, Claire climbs into his Pathfinder with a litre of Club Soda, sipping as Brian drives. Brian hates carbonated beverages and will not ask for a taste. Good thing, as it is generously laced with vodka, though Claire is not sure why she dashed back to the apartment—on the pretense of changing her shoes—in order to secure the drink. She believes herself outgoing and cannot blame the urge on nervousness. And it certainly wasn't a liquor craving, *per se*. She decrees her secret sipping as a mere decadence, a lark, to take the monotony out of the long drive.

There are cocktails waiting on the patio after the niceties are exchanged. Brian has one but leaves half of it; his father, mother, and Claire have two. Claire glugs the rest of Brian's when she helpfully takes the glasses to the kitchen. They all drink wine with dinner, and Claire feels herself dropping off at only eight, so she accepts a double-espresso from Brian's father and chases it with the proffered Courvousier. She has never drunk Courvousier; what a civilized drink.

Brian's mother drinks copious amounts of the cognac and is ushered off to bed at around ten, when she becomes boisterous and commences asking Claire embarrassing questions about their sex life and how much money she makes. Brian is mortified.

"Dad told me she quit," he hisses at Claire as his mother is being propelled upstairs. "That's the only reason I finally brought you here. I could kill him. And her."

"Don't worry about it, Brian," soothes Claire, feeling very milky and loose herself. "It's a disease; she can't help it."

At least I don't get drunk. Not drunk, drunk. I never get drunk like that.

Brian tells Claire about the time when he was ten or eleven, and caught his mother filling up the vodka bottle with water. She said she was cleaning it out, but it was back in the high cupboard over the sink, three-quarters full, when he later checked.

Claire tenses and stares at the little red buttons dripping down Brian's denim shirt.

The buttons stare back.

"And another time," continues Brian, though Claire wants to shout at him to stop telling her tricks and secrets, "when I was about sixteen, I had a friend over and we were going to try out this drinking thing—you know, typical teenage shit. All there was in The Cupboard—my father always spoke it like it was capitalized, if you know what I mean: 'Suzanne, The Cupboard's empty again' or 'Suzanne, I've emptied The Cupboard'. Anyway, all that was there looked to be rye, but it turned out to be diluted apple juice."

Claire has never quite felt this combination of revulsion, pity, and interest before.

In the morning, she forces herself up earlier than Brian and gulps down two mimosas and three Tylenol with his parents. Nothing is said about the previous evening.

Thank God. Who wants to hear some rich bitch blathering out excuses for being a lush, anyway?

Claire borrows a mickey of gin from The Cupboard for the drive home while the others are touring the gardens. To make sure it is unbastardized, she takes a nip and is rewarded with the searing, first-sip rush that she craves.

Three weeks later, she receives a juicy contract to renovate a theatre lobby, and she takes her favourite colleagues out for cocktails. It was a fun night, Claire is certain, but is irritated when she wakes up and it is not clear how she got from the downtown pub to her apartment on East 122nd Avenue. All she can do in the morning is give a little groan-giggle.

At least there is no strange man beside me.

That would indicate a definite problem. The concept makes her giggle more before she must rush to the bathroom and puke what feels like her guts out.

Then Brian, who is getting a little tedious with his desire for wholesome entertainment like squash and walks on the boardwalk, goes out of town on business. Unfortunately, he goes with her purse in the trunk of his car, because she hadn't wanted to take it into the Grizzlies game the night before—the live basketball game during which she actually fell asleep, even amid the Electropop of the Extreme Dance Team and screaming fans. When Brian elbowed her hard enough, she'd grimly decided to tell the Crown Royal people to add some caffeine to their concoction.

Consequently, she now has this purse/cash/credit card problem. He will only be gone for three days and there is milk, bread, eggs, and other staples in her fridge, so she'll not starve. She knows this. She also has a dinner coupon for Mama Josie's Family Pasta Emporium, but it's not bloody licensed, so why bother? Besides, there are people to borrow cash from, if she gets that desperate.

She won't get that desperate.

It's nine o'clock on the first night, a Tuesday, and no one Claire calls for companionship is home or available. There is nothing on TV. She feels restless. Anxious, even. She wishes for a video and a bottle of wine to pass the evening, and ends up smashing open the ceramic change box her niece made.

Stupid to make it without an opening, save the tiny slit for the coins.

Within the lame little fan-out of coins the destruction creates, there are zero twonies, three loonies, a couple of quarters, and lots of dimes and nickels. She fills her pockets with handfuls of even-dollar amounts, and sets out.

At the off-licence, she stands in a queue consisting of two young guys with beer, a well-dressed woman cuddling champagne, and a scruffy man smothering the cheapest red wine going.

Does he have pink elephants written all over him, or what?

Claire casually holds a small flask of gin, not recalling if off-sales incorporated the bottle deposit or not.

When it's her turn to pay, Claire accidentally drops the second handful of forty nickels and ten dimes; they scatter and she is holding up the line behind her. In a loud voice, Claire announces to the entire store that she is *most* sorry and how she should have used her debit card, but she wanted to get rid of all the weighty change from various coat pockets.

Blah, blah, blah.

Who is that talking, anyway? The clerk looks at her blankly and starts re-counting the coins Claire retrieves from the sticky, gritty linoleum and from between the various impatiently shunting feet. The bum wears pumpkin-orange high-tops with no laces; the socialite, pearly slingbacks. The tiles are flecked with green, blue, yellow, and washed-out red. Claire is right there, inches away, so she knows.

She ends up forty-five cents short—some coins have apparently rolled under the ice machine—so the scruffy man, who has been hovering in the doorway since jumping the queue and paying, gives her fifty cents. Directly behind her, the coiffed lady takes a step back and meets no one's eyes. The college boys are long gone.

Claire thanks Mr. Scruffy in a retarded voice, like he doesn't comprehend English, and scuttles out of the store and back to the safety of her apartment as quickly as she can, where there will be no one to make false assumptions.

Since she hadn't scraped enough together for the video, Claire is stuck with inane comedy or American news shows. She thinks about Scruffy Man, drinking in an alley somewhere, or under one of the Georgia Strait bridges, where she assumes the winos hang out. At best, he is holed up in one of those shady men's hostels. Poor bastard. The college boys are probably playing caps for fifty cents a pop in lieu of studying for their sports med tests; the snobby lady has toasted whatever it is she is celebrating and is now eating the fancy catered canapés. Something like that, anyway. And she, Claire, eventually, at least when she's two glasses down, she will be a freewheeling gal watching Nick at Night.

One glass per rerun allowed.

Okay, two.

The next morning, Claire drinks coffee at her kitchen table and eyes the empty gin bottle lying on the counter. Also, she discovers she has spilled ketchup on her cream-coloured raw-silk couch at some point during the night and is disproportionately peeved.

She feels too weak to tackle the wounded couch, but does manage to clean up the remains of the desecrated ceramic coin box, having been in too much of a hurry last night to do anything but kick the bigger chunks to one side.

Claire swears and sucks off the bead of blood that appears on the pad of her finger, pricked by a pointy shard. Up it pops again, a bulbous, quivering red eye.

She thinks about Brian's mother, boring old dead Geoff, Maggie's control, the firmness in the voice of the man with the Diet Coke. Claire shuffles into the kitchen, paws through drawers and junk baskets until she finds a pen and notepad, then sits and brainstorms.

She lists eighteen strange drinking behaviours, rituals, and manipulations in less than ten minutes. The list makes her feel very uncomfortable.

Very un-normal.

She gets out the Yellow Pages, just to see; she catches herself wishing for the tiniest of sips, the slightest of buzzes. It would come so easy on her empty stomach.

At 7:05 this same evening, Claire stands outside an auditorium door in a questionable suburb in which she knows not a soul. Already tense, she almost bolts when the door creaks open. There are twenty-five people or so inside. Their chairs are gathered in a semicircle around a battered old desk. Behind the desk sits someone reading from a blue paperback. The hall is cold and most still wear their overcoats—a grenadine-red leather bomber, a Curaco-blue ski jacket, a Grand Marnier-yellow slicker, a milky-brown Irish Cream trench coat. Eight faces turn and look for the source of the creak, then smile and motion her in.

Claire shakes her head and leans against the back wall.

"At this time, we'd like to welcome any visiting members or newcomers," announces the man at the desk. "Are there any visitors from out of town?"

The lady saturated in grenadine holds up her hand. "I'm Rachel and I'm an alcoholic, in town on business from Edmonton, and am I ever grateful for this meeting here tonight."

"Welcome, Rachel," everyone choruses.

Claire's hands are stuck together, poised over her sloshing stomach. The man at the desk is going to look at her and expect her to say something. It feels likes a corkscrew's twisting into her Adam's apple.

"And newcomers? Miss? In the back? Don't worry; you don't have to speak, but please tell us your first name so that we can get to know you better."

Claire drops her head. Fifty eyes are looking at her. Fifty evil red pimentos. She briefly squeezes hers shut. *God help me*, she accidentally prays. When she opens them, unbelievingly, the tableau is more unbearable than she imagined: all eyes gaze at her like a cocker spaniel's, steady and kind.

"Claire," she croaks out. "My name is Claire."

She is about to add that she is not sure that she should even be here, that it is not really that much of a problem, but everyone singsongs, "Welcome, Claire. Welcome," before she can qualify herself.

And the man at the desk says, "Yes, welcome, Claire. May you find what you seek."

A chair between a university sweatshirt of crème de menthe green and a sturdy corduroy car coat in malt is earnestly offered to Claire. She shakes her head. To sit would make them equals.

god. damn. it. i. am. not. like. you.

She chastises herself for her panic, her overreaction to one bad night, one kind of bad night, and fights the urge to flee. No need to be rude to the poor sods.

At the break time, after some gobbledy-gook about rigorous honesty and Higher Powers, Claire bolts out the door and down the street to avoid having to insult anyone and explain her premature concern.

When she reaches the corner, she slows her gait and checks her pockets for money, one more time. Of course, there is nothing. There is nothing.

Then she thinks of Chad, an old boyfriend. He lives very close. Yes.

Yes!

Now Chad, *he* was a boozer. With a growing urgency, Claire starts walking toward his townhouse, maybe ten blocks away. Maybe more. Whatever. For a little flirtation, maybe a few promising kisses, Chad will be happy to crack open a little something.

Jumping Off

The first thing I notice when I climb in my sister's car is that she's wearing the denim shirt I gave her for Christmas at least five years ago. The second thing's the huge, tacky gas-station air freshener, hooked over the rearview mirror. Waning spearmint.

She says *hi* with what I interpret as false cheeriness, and that's what my response is laced with. But she nobly manages to add, "I'm glad you decided to come, Vicky."

Oof. Next might come a hug.

"Please don't call me Vicky."

"You spent over twenty-five years not answering to anything else," Sharyn reminds me. She is thirty-nine, a year older than me. People described us as 'curds and whey' when we were little. Dithery old aunts still do, and it's a fair enough call. I've certainly always thought of Sharyn as watery, with a chalky, translucent quality. Me, I work hard at keeping my rind thick and rationing out myself in expensive slivers. As if she, too, is thinking about our differences, she says, "You look funny."

And you look utterly content.

"Funny ha-ha, or funny peculiar?"

"Different. What is it?" She scrutinizes me, and I wait for her inevitable pounce. "Oh, my God! Your eyes! Since when do you have brown eyes?"

Suddenly I feel ridiculous, caught in a lie. Again. "Hey, they're 'Swiss Chocolate' and they cost 322 bucks, so do you mind?"

We drive on in silence for a few blocks. Though for different reasons than Sharyn was imagining, I must have sighed and pinched up my face, because she comments, "Look, if you don't want to do this, ya snob," and she was only half-teasing—"just forget it."

"I do want to. Sorry." I refocus. The next bit is said to cover my motivations for meeting her. "You know me; I'm just used to Robson Street, not . . ."

"Value Village," she finishes for me and cranks her '86 Topaz left, from Boundary onto Hastings. I swear we two-wheel it. "I just wanted to do something together. If you don't want to do it for me, do it to get Mom off your case."

Our Mom is dying. Lung cancer. Her final wish is for peace between her two offspring.

"A good reason, yes, but I'll do it because I want to spend time with you, too." True? I'm in no condition to judge black, white, or shades of gray right now.

"Well, okay, but this is spending time with me." She chuckles, which I find amazing. "It's this, baseball with Chad, chasing Jeff around to keep his retainer in, or banging at a calculator paying the bills with Lorne. Take your pick."

Lorne, the brother-in-law I kissed, just because, while Sharyn was in the kitchen serving out lasagna. Another of my 'seemed like a good idea at the time' acts. The air in the car is suddenly thick, like breathing sawdust, even though the windows are open.

She pulls into the parking lot of Value Village. Four lost souls are sifting through the back alley rejects, the junk that didn't even make it into the second-hand store. They are the really broken ones.

"You know, Vicky, I don't know if this is pure jealousy talking or what, but you really have to get off your high horse; there're fabulous buys in here."

I make a whinny sound.

"Very funny. Very clever. Of course, you have that big degree and all. I can't compete, with my little old bookkeeping diploma." She is still speaking lightly, but we have begun.

I plunge us five levels down with my cutting tone. "If you hate my company so much, why did you beg me to come with you?"

Never ask a question if you don't want to know the answer.

She looks at me, her spotty face perplexed. "Because I always hope things will be different, don't you?"

"We haven't gotten along since we were eleven and twelve; why would now be different?" I bump us down another nasty level.

"Jesus, sometimes you're a bitch, Vicky. How do you snag all those big clients for the hotel, being such a bag?"

Work. Shit.

"I don't want to talk about work."

"Really? You always want to talk about work. 'My job is this, my job is that. I got a promotion, I shook hands with Martin Sheen, I hired somebody to wipe my butt.' You always want to talk about work; why not now? Didn't get the 20 per cent raise this quarter?"

I usually feel smugness at this point, knowing I have sucked her down, once again, and we've settled into our push-and-pull relationship.

Instead, I say calmly, "Can we just drop it?" Two beats. "Please."

She cocks her head and regards me. "Fine. Take a taxi home if you want. This outing was a mistake, mine entirely. Feel free to go, wait in the car, whatever."

I sigh. I am a bitch. A lot of the time. Usually it works for me.

I respond by groping the side of the seat for the recline handle, finding it, and yanking. The bucket seat goes back farther than I expect and I am practically prone, like at a dentist's. Or a shrink's. There are holes, slashes, and remnants of McFlurries in the vinyl ceiling. I close my eyes to them. I hear Sharyn get out, slam the door.

Alone in the minty-smelling Topaz, my heart starts thudding, my stomach convulsing. This, *this* is why I came with her to this stupid second-hand shop. I cannot be still right now and stay alive. I cannot be alone and there is no one else.

My colleagues have been instructed by legal counsel not to communicate with me.

I will not draw in my social acquaintances at this juncture. Never, if possible.

There is a mother, wracked by pain and floating on megadoses of morphine, or a chalky sister who is everything I am not. Ironically, this is a good thing.

A man taps at the driver's side window, and I jolt back to life. He wants to know if the car is coming or going, wants the parking space. I frown and shake my head, pointing to the absence of a driver. He stomps away, climbs back in his double-parked truck, and guns off.

I heave myself out of the car because I have to.

Inside the store, the air is musty, like waiting in an old cardboard box during Hide and Seek, terrified of being found.

One cashier on duty has fascinating hair. It is dozens, hundreds, of tiny braids in various shades of blue. It fuzzes around the crown. Plus, I have never seen anyone with a stud across the bridge of the nose like that. Positively barbaric.

I find Sharyn near the front of the store, in the accessories department. Beside her, two girls with Australian twangs laugh over a garish scarf on which is printed a caricatured map of their country.

I know that I need to make peace. Soon, Sharyn will be all there is. Still, I search for wounding words that I can later claim as pure jest.

"Hey," I joke, wiggling the pant leg of an engine-red snowsuit at her. "Isn't this yours, from third grade? Let's see if the pee stain is still there from when Bobby McLaren sat on you to wash your face in the snow."

She grins cheerily and I am irked. I meant to offend, to dig, to remind her of shameful past days, since she will not be shamed for who she is now.

I prowl around, trying to out-maneuver a body that betrays me with its shudders and cramps. In the kitchen section, I finger Hawaiian teak peanut dishes and remember Mom's, filled with mixed nuts. Sharyn and I would sneak into the living room before the adult party and pilfer the cashews and almonds. Guests, in swishy black palazzo pants and polyester blazers, were forced to choose between oily peanuts and bland Brazil nuts. We double-dared each other to call them nigger toes, back then.

I exclaim at the equally retro clunky ceramic onion soup bowls, chocolate brown with white, heavily lacquered drizzles all over. Four bucks a set. They lie next to various K-tel products and across from festive biscuit tins.

I circle the store twice before stopping at Sharyn again, in the men's T-shirts section.

"Where is that kid's mother?" I hiss, frowning at a grubby ten-year-old playing a harmonica. I am attempting to appeal to her maternal instincts, which, from what I have seen during my sporadic visits to suburbia, are solid and just. "My God, who knows where that mouthpiece has been."

"Whatever," she answers impatiently. "I'm sure it's nothing worse than what's in the air we all breathe."

"Jesus," I say, miffed. "Since when did you become so blasé about the evils of germs? You used to walk around with a spritz-bottle of Lysol all the time."

"When your husband gets fired for blowing the whistle on corrupt management about the same time your pitiful stocks nose-dive, so you start shopping at the Payless Meat store, hoping like heck your ground round came from an ugly animal and is considered appropriate for eating by the Health Act, that's when." She circulates to the back of the store. We pass the underwear and bathing suits and I think, before I can stop myself, *How grotesque. Second-hand underwear?*

I didn't know this about Lorne, but it figures. Lorne, who'd shoved me off him in goddamn horror as Sharyn dished up dinner, is a man of principle. Shitty taste, but principle. I want to ask more about what exactly his managers were up to, but she keeps talking.

"Listen, I know it's a few months off, but do you know what

you'll be doing for Christmas? Let's be real; it's going to be Mom's last Christmas. Are you going to be here, or off chugging Bahama Mamas, like last year?"

I open and close my mouth. Unlike the kid's mouth organ, no sound is emitted. Christmas seems so incredibly far in the future. I could wake up from this nightmare by then or I could be some dyke's prison toy, so I don't answer.

Now the kid with the harmonica is jumping off the stairs that lead to the second floor, which presumably houses all the admin crap. The harmonica is still jammed in his mouth. I want to shake him, lecture him about running with scissors and lollipops. He climbs two steps, wheezes out a few harsh notes, and jumps down. He repeats this for the third step. At the bottom, he removes the organ, wipes his mouth on his sleeve, and goes again. He is wearing skookum sneakers and makes a soft thud when he lands.

Suddenly, the stale air progresses to suffocating. I lap the premises again, faster than before, trying to find pockets of oxygen, but there are none.

I have fucked up so bigtime, I cannot comprehend it.

I grip the end of a coat rack for support, but it's not secure and shunts against my weight, so I stumble into a bin of polyester ties, almost overturning it.

Behind me, the little boy is halfway up the stairs. He paces back and forth, wheezing away into his goddamned harmonica.

"Will you shut the hell up?" I shriek up the stairs, resenting his frivolous use of my air. He stops. The whole store stops, it seems. Peripherally, I see Shar. She stares at me from two rows of faded fabrics over, but doesn't come to me. In fact, she tilts her head and scrunches up her face in disassociation.

Ha, it seems to be saying. *Who's embarrassing who, now?*

I split apart. Like a strip of rotting material. One half, the half that stood in front of my boss, Leonard, yesterday morning, screams, "Why are you doing this to me?" in melodramatic outrage. The other half panics—perches on the edge of the Brighton Park swimming pool and refuses to dive into the arms of a daddy who will shortly throw himself off the Pattulo Bridge.

Been trying to make up for that by showing off ever since.

The boy stares down at me; the instrument flashes at me like gargantuan braces. Saliva drips out the corners of his mouth. I face him as I retreat, like he might jump me from behind if I turn my back, then head to the front of the store to escape. The first aisle is blocked by an obese woman, her cart full not of treasures, but of cinnamon-coloured children with black flashing eyes, shiny with excitement. Like a handful of worms, they squirm and stretch over each other, unable to break out of their cage.

I back up and try the next aisle over, my panic to get out of the store ever increasing. On the floor of the next aisle sit two teenagers with piles of long, formal gowns between them. I plow through, manic, kicking one of the girls in the process, then trip over the mound of garments that wrap around my ankles like shackles.

I feel myself falling, and reach out wildly to cling to something to keep me up, but the clothes I grab slip off their hangers and I end up clutching air that doesn't sustain me.

The tile floor is cool against my hot cheeks and for a moment, I am blissful. Then, the humiliation sets in and I begin to cry.

We lie, the garish swatches and I, in a discombobulated pile. The girls, horrified, scoot away.

Now I am sobbing. I think one of my contacts has popped out, and I visualize the freakish look that one chocolate eye and one pale hazel eye must create.

Sharyn comes running from the other end of the aisle, electric-blue bell-bottoms clutched in her left hand.

"My God! What happened?"

I have become aware of my weeping and I attempt to stop, but this only increases its intensity. I have no choice but to lie there, askew, letting the waves of hysteria slosh over me.

"I'm fine," I manage to heave, as another bucket of fear and shame is poured over my head. I feel a tugging. One of the girls is trying to retrieve a dress I hold captive under my legs.

"Sorry," she says in a strangulated whisper. "I want to try on this yellow one."

For some reason, I find this incredibly funny and begin laughing through my convulsions. I lift my legs high in the air, a beetle on its back, and she cautiously retrieves the yards of taffeta.

"Vicky! What is the matter with you?" Sharyn asks again, more gently, and squats besides me. "Are you hurt? If not, will you get up, already? People are looking."

I giggle. "My worst nightmare."

I look to either end and acknowledge my motley audience. A man in baggy khakis, the waistband hovering at crotch level, stands beside a heavily tattooed youth with an orange mohawk. Two teeny Asian girls huddle at the other end, their arms intertwined, murmuring back and forth.

"Yes," I assure them loudly, "I am one of those Western spectacles you may have heard about. No saving face for this boorish broad." They shoot rapid Cantonese back and forth.

Suddenly, I feel drunk and tired, and I now want to hide, but the exit from the place where I am seems so very far away.

Sharyn says, "I'll just put these back, get my other stuff, and we can go. Okay?"

I wave at her limply. The employee on duty at the change rooms is bald but for a single, floppy curl of downy black hair that wisps off the top of his head. Like a baby's. He wears the store's signature red smock, undone at the sides. I crawl past him and haul myself into a cubicle. My feet stick out under the door.

How did this happen? How did I go from a six-figure salary, cocktail parties, and men who brought jewelry as token gifts, to sitting on a pockmarked tiled floor, sticky with spilled soda and God knows what else, staring into the back of a pressboard door with teenage love-messages scrawled on it?

How indeed.

I sigh, overwhelmed.

In a few minutes, Sharyn yanks open the door and stares down at me. She doesn't need to ask again.

"What the fuck," I slur. "You're going to find out soon enough. I got fired yesterday."

She gasps.

"Yup. Canned. Given my walking papers. Handed the pink slip. All of the above."

"But why? You were the top agent. Look at all the sales awards you got."

"It's complicated."

"Try me."

I don't look at her. Can't. I imagine her pinky-white rabbit nose, quivering in anticipation. "I didn't exactly follow the rules."

"You cheated the hotel?"

"At the beginning, I guess it'd be called cheating. I'd bump contract dates around, make some promises I knew couldn't be kept, to make the numbers look better for the month. At the end . . ."

"At the end . . ." she prompts.

My throat is stinging; I don't know if I can get it out.

"Vic?"

"I'm being criminally charged." I can barely hear myself. "With embezzlement, among other things."

"Holy."

"Smoly," I finish automatically, a throwback to the days when we were more in tune with each other.

"But why? Why would you do such a thing?" I read in her face a combination of horror and fascination. Perhaps also glee. I refuse to acknowledge the pity.

"I don't know. It got kind of addictive after a while, seeing what could be pulled off, and of course, the money."

"But we all thought you were so great," she says bluntly, then covers her mouth. "Sorry. You know what I mean." She shifts her position. "Actually, it's a relief to me." Right before my eyes, she is toughening and thickening as if rennet is being added to her milky character as we speak. "Do you want me to be there when you talk to Mom?"

"Mom? Are you kidding? She's the last person I'd tell. Give the woman a break."

"Give her a break is right! Victoria, she has cancer, not myopia or Alzheimer's. You have to tell her, in case someone else does. If you came and saw her more, you'd see how strong she is. Besides, you'll live with far greater guilt if she dies with you the centre of a ridiculous lie."

On the other side of the door, two huge Converse sneakers appear, straddling my outstretched legs. There is a sharp knock. "Hello? We have a lineup here. What's the holdup?"

Sharyn bangs back. "Don't worry; we're having a breakdown, not layering ourselves in your shit clothes to steal."

I laugh. I didn't know she had it in her. Then again, she didn't miss her chance to dive, so many years ago.

"Vicky, how'd you get in so deep?"

I mutter something about the echo in the cubicle, and deem her question rhetorical. It's not our style to get mushy, so Sharyn doesn't reach for me, or even hold my hand. She clicks her tongue though, and nods thoughtfully.

From the back of the store, the harmonica is honked from high above us. A beat, and then I hear the thud of sneakers hitting the floor.

Acknowledgements

My sincere thanks to the NeWest Board for choosing *Jumping Off* for publication and to Ruth, Erin and David in the office for making it actually happen; to Dr. Lynne Van Luven for her valuable editing and help in polishing each storyline, each character, not to mention Christine Savage for her eagle-eyed copy-editing. Also, I thank my family and friends who squealed with delight or simply offered a heartfelt "Cool!" when I announced the acceptance of a second collection.

Laura Cutler has had careers as a hotel manager and an RCMP officer, and has traveled on six continents. *Jumping Off* is her second published collection of short stories. Her stories have also been published in anthologies, including the *North (Vancouver) Shore Writer's Association Millenium Anthology*, and Indigo Books/Henkell Trocken's *What the Henkell Happened Here?* Cutler currently lives in Calgary, Alberta, where, when not 37,000 feet in the air being a flight attendant, she writes and hands out dog cookies.